OVER THE HILLS:

The Welsh great Escape

by

Nigel Barley

To: Cornelia and Friedrich

Krummes Holz gibt auch gerades Feuer (hoffentlich)

ISBN: 9781676646204
First published 2020
Copyright Nigel Barley
The moral right of the author is asserted

Introduction

Everyone has heard of The Great Escape from the books written about it or the sensational film – its Britishness as clipped as a railway ticket - without whose screening on television no Christmas would once have been complete. In March 1944, seventy-six mainly British and Commonwealth airmen tunnelled out of the PoW camp, Stalag Luft III, in Poland and escaped, triggering a vast manhunt throughout occupied Europe. Of the seventy-three subsequently recaptured, forty-one were shot by the SS in cold blood on the personal orders of Adolf Hitler and this atrocity sent shockwaves through the nation and resulted in a relentless search after the end of hostilities for those responsible. The incident became an icon of British decency in the face of Nazi barbarity.

Yet only a year later, seventy German prisoners of war, including SS officers, returned the compliment by constructing a very similar tunnel to escape from Island Farm PoW camp in Wales. The two cases, superficially so similar, could not have been more different. While the complex ingenuities of British prisoners in Germany have been heavily documented, historical attention to the Welsh breakout has focused almost entirely on the very British search for the escapees that followed this event, a sort of cross between Dad's Army and an Ealing comedy, full of good intentions and pratfalls that baffled both sides and prompted several books and an official enquiry.

More generally, while the literature on British PoWs, both official and personal, is enormous, virtually nothing has been written on the experiences of German prisoners who fell into Allied hands, the only exception being of those that were interned in the United States and felt the full-fat impact of their shattering encounter with the candy floss and ice-cream economy of America after the harsh austerities of wartime Europe. So, the German PoW experience of British captivity has largely been deleted from historical consciousness.

While the present work is to be seen as one of fiction, revisiting that basic Welsh event and drawing on information about other camps and conflating other escapes to fill out these gaps in our knowledge, virtually nothing here has been wholly invented and even many of the characters were much as described here. It is significant that, after it was all over, doubts remained over exactly how many men had got through the wire and even whether or not they had all been accounted for.

Nigel Barley

CHAPTER ONE

'Aargh!' Billy Jones received the bullet in his chest and clutched both hands to the fatal wound, his face contorted with sudden agony and the terrible knowledge of the inevitability of his own death. His thick, black hair – too long uncut – flopped over his young features as he crumpled slowly from the knees, twisting as he toppled and fell face down onto the cushioning leaf mould of the forest, one skinny leg shooting out to twitch in a final spasm as body and soul parted company, one arm flung forward as if reaching for some final truth to carry over into the next world or launching a last vengeful grenade against his killers. A hole in the sole of his shoe had been blocked with a piece of old, parquet-patterned lino and was now tragically revealed, together with an undarned patch in the heel of one sock. There came a final exhalation, the death rattle in the throat, and it was all over. Schoolboy Billy was dead.

He sat up, grinning with artistic pride and wiped dirt from his mouth. Leaf mould was not his preferred surface for dying on. Grass was infinitely better but these days a performer had go to with whatever props lay to hand. 'Now <u>that's</u> how you die when the Jerries shoot you. I've seen it at the flicks.'

The other boys – Jimmy, Fred and Arthur– gathered round and nodded in admiration, their tommy gun sticks tucked over arms and pointed safely at the ground in proper military fashion. There was that famous picture of Winnie posing with one in a striped suit, a tough-guy cigar in his mouth, looking for all the world like Al Capone out to spread some heat. Billy was a Class A hero. He'd been the first to swing across the stream on the end of a rope like Tarzan the Ape Man, the first to find a way into the American army camp through the barbed wire and the first to charm the twinkling jewel of a real live bullet out of the troops on their way to D-Day. But now they were gone, reduced to mere stark reports on the wireless, and Bridgend had gone back to being the dead boring sort of hole it had always been before the war, a place divorced from the wider world of events where nothing ever happened.

Billy picked up his tommy gun stick and rose from the dead, feeling the burden of leadership heavy on his slim shoulders.

'We could go and check the haystacks for German paratroopers.' They were known to seek them out for soft landings and hiding places so that jumping up and down on them and messing them up was a patriotic act.

Jimmy Taylor sighed. 'They're all fighting in France. There ain't none here.'

It was true, the moment for German parachutists had passed.

'There are still loads of spies.'

They had their eye on Miss Gilbert, the post mistress, who was not quite Welsh and had strung out a suspiciously long metal washing line that might easily be used as a radio aerial for sending secrets across the Channel or over to the thousands of German agents known to be lurking in Ireland. They had spied on her by day and night, climbed into the tree outside her bedroom window and discovered that she wore no drawers under her tweed skirts in summer. Stringent clothes rationing had led to all manner of innovations in dress but this was clearly an important truth about her basic respectability - though one that could not easily be shared.

'I reckon they've all run off too.' Fred was a nervous boy whose dad had not run off and so been killed in a blasted tank in North Africa. They speculated endlessly on just how. Arthur's father was never mentioned. It was rumoured that he had been 'inside' and benefitted from some scheme to turn convicts into soldiers in exchange for commutation of their sentence. Billy's own virtuous father was guarding the grey Orkneys with a rifle and three rounds of ammunition. Once he had seen a German submarine off the coast - or it could have been a whale – no one was quite sure but they had fired at it anyway and been appalled by the paperwork so generated. The lesson had been learned. They would not fire another shot for the length of the war. Billy was grateful to know he was safe but slightly embarrassed by the absence of any claim to heroism in defending the world against fish.

'What about the main road and stupid travellers.' They could always position themselves at the main junction and ambush lost motorists with wild-eyed innocence. With all the road signs taken down to confuse the Jerries who never even bothered to come after all, everyone was permanently lost and asking directions and you could have great fun sending them off on entirely the wrong track with the added spice of danger that they might come back seeking revenge for all that wasted petrol and chase you.

'Boring! Anyway, we got caught last week and PC Gifford'll give us a right belting and tell our parents if he catches us at it again.' Jimmy's dad was a preacher, ever ready to help out divinity and the law by handing out God's punishment with a leather belt.

'We could go scrumping...No, wait it's still too early. Nothing will be ripe.' Even the posh people's greenhouses would offer slim pickings. Billy looked glum and kicked at a tree stump. With the insight of any great leader, he saw where the threat to his position was coming from. It was important his men should not realise how dull life was under his command. He brightened. In a comic, an illuminated light bulb would have appeared over his head.

'Let's go to the camp and muck it up. It's completely empty now.'

The camp was still a place of promise even without the glamorous American soldiers with their easy ways, strange underwear, chewing gum, music and candy bars, men who laughed like drains when you expressed surprise at anything by saying, 'Well, blow me!' There would be abandoned dirty magazines offering mysteries to be pored over, windows to be smashed, doors to be booted in, water fights to be had as you ran screaming up and down the corridors. It was a fine substitute for the thrilling bomb sites of their sneery urban cousins in Swansea.

'Yeah!'

The British have always had a hesitant relationship with water and, after the battered, lick-and-a-promise grunginess of British troops, the Americans were perhaps the first really clean people the boys had ever seen, toothily toothsome, a gleaming credit to Pepsodent and Brylcreem. They smelled, not of the mildew and stale armpits that lingeringly permeated the known world, but of mum's best soap, kept for special. Milk-fed and shiny with untarnished youth, they exuded optimism and laughter and it soon emerged that they were paid five times as much as their downtrodden British counterparts. British adult resentment and envy crystalised in their description as 'overpaid, oversexed and over here' which elicited the American response that their British allies were 'underpaid, undersexed and under Eisenhower'.

The high point of relations had been a Christmas party thrown for the open-mouthed, local children with a tree decorated with the aluminium chaff used to confuse German radar - jellies, cakes, games and a Father Christmas with a real Aw Shucks American accent. Even in everyday life their arms were always full of spam, chocolate, coffee and other almost forgotten luxuries that they dispensed with careless generosity and the boys fell in love with them at once - as did their grown-up sisters – as creatures from another world and a land of milk and Hershey. Several boys cultivated American accents and carefully referred to their kecks as 'pants' to general laughter, a confusion that, among the female population, probably explained an outbreak of swollen bellies among the unmarried.

There were plenty of black troops too, of course, but they were tucked away, several miles down the road, living scarily amongst windblown woodsmoke in camouflaged tents that stood out brightly against the contrasting sand dunes and not to be officially visited on any account except by preachers. There had been fights with the white GIs at dances and they had been ordered to keep their distance but the thick scatter of contraceptives slowly shrivelling across the dunes suggested they had not lacked for company. The boys were not convinced by stories that they were used to keep salt water out of rifle barrels during military landing exercises and had carefully observed these exotic beings from afar. They were fascinated by the first black faces they had ever seen and been unable to work out their place in the structure of the world, their subjection contradicted by their lavish equipment and easy, loose-limbed ways. At night, they could be heard singing and clapping just like the Africans in 'Sanders of the River'. They decided they were too dangerous to approach.

They put their sticks over their shoulders and marched off full of happy anticipation, Billy at their head.

'Left, right. Left, right.'

He turned and watched them following him with the despair familiar to all drill sergeants. It was painfully clear that Fred still didn't know which foot was which.

◆ ◆ ◆

The army camp had been planned as a dormitory for the biggest factory ever built, Royal Ordnance factory 53. Opened a year before the outbreak of war with fanfares of trumpets, it was top secret and originally intended to produce ammunition for what many now regarded as an inevitable conflict and supplement the production of Woolwich Arsenal which was suddenly realised to be conveniently situated for bombing raids from continental Europe. With the fall of France and weapons of longer range than a 19th-century cannon, the move was made unfortunately pointless as the new factory was now just as vulnerable as the old one to bombers operating from bases there. Immediately, a local legend sprang up that it was protected by some sort of magical, Celtic mist like dragon's breath, that welled up from the ground at the approach of a German bomber to blend with the industrial smoke from above and clasp the works in conferred invisibility. The fact was that it was foolishly built on marshy ground and highly unsuitable for the vast tunnelling and underground construction work that was required for production and storage. Only constant pumping kept it free from flooding. The plant ingested a daily diet of 40,000 workers and contained its own hospital, police force and fire station and its terror of German bombs was only equalled by the fear of sparks caused by hairpins which the nation's best scientists had declared a worrying theoretical possibility. For the general workers were to be notoriously giddy young women in their teens and twenties, gathered in from surrounding villages to be trained up in the dangerous manufacture and filling of shells. It was good steady money in a depressed area and far more than their husbands got in heavy industry or farming, undermining many a domestic hierarchy as relentlessly as the miners undermined the nearby coal seams. The only bother was the yellow dye they added to the cordite so you could see it if it had got where it shouldn't and the choking sulphur and poisonous - potentially lethal - fumes from the TNT. Since these effects were never explained to the girls, they were much more concerned with the way work in the factory turned your hands and face yellow so kids called you 'Canary girl' and, if the toxins got into your hair, blond went green and black became a very nasty shade of red.

The hundred-odd Nissen huts of the separate camp – male planners thought - would spare them a long and tedious bus journey, inefficiently back and forth every day, between the factory and their damp, cold hovels in the surrounding towns and villages. For the hours were long, work required concentration, any inattention could cause an accident – a shell dropped, a fuse triggered - unleashing devastating consequences only hinted at by the massive containing walls, deliberately weak roofs to allow the upward dissipation of explosions, and the high earth banks piled around the buildings. The planners ignored the fact that the girls were unused to factory life with its relentless production lines that were constantly notched up to increase output so it was the bus journey that was the best part of their day. The homeward journey universally started with a long, languorous drag on a welcome gateside fag that was forbidden on site and so became the mark of final liberation once they had sloughed off the obligatory overalls, turban and rubber overshoes that reduced them from humans to faceless abattoir workers.   On the buses, the women swiftly developed a sense of fellowship, twittering and gossiping happily with an energy unseen on the production lines. It was all innocent enough. There were knitting contests - who could produce the longest scarf in the course of the journey - singing competitions between different sides of the bus or different villages and discreet racing along the windswept country lanes between honking charabancs. They chattered about life, their hardships, their hopeless boyfriends, hapless husbands and cheeky children and fervently debated the relative sexual attractiveness of film stars and male workers at the plant with whoops and blushes. Yet, with their ancient skills of class-resentment and envy, they somehow always retained plenty of time for cursing the foremen, the overseers and the canteen food, the war and the Germans and 'Music While You Work' played on the bloody banjo - with tongue-tipped swearwords. It was like those jolly summer bus trips to the seaside organised by village before the whole world changed and everything became about the war. To lose all this and freeze to death in a grim hostel of ugly, concrete slabs where the outside fog lurked in the corners even on sunny days, would be like being in prison. They perished the thought, which left the bleak camp available as a telling example of what might happen if the civilisation they
were told they were fighting to save should collapse and be swept away. This had luckily made it available for the US troops streaming in for the invasion of Europe.

8

♦ ♦ ♦

'What's going on? Are the Yanks back then?'

But there was no Yankee slickness here and these were old, British trucks and British troops in crumpled battledress. The boys peered through the blackberry bushes from across the road where lorries were milling around the gate that was still decorated with glamorous signs threatening instant death to all trespassers. One board was being taken down and replaced with another, a job that seemed to require the skills of one sergeant, two corporals and six men. They strained their eyes to read it in the pale sunshine that seemed as if it too had been watered down for rationing purposes. 'Island Farm PoW Camp 198.'

They looked at each other with raised eyebrows.

'What's PoW?'

'The sound of someone being bashed. Pow! Take that Kraut!' Fred demonstrated with a vicious punch to thin air. 'Like in the comics. Must be special forces.' The others muttered and shook their heads. That was too good to be true.

'Could be short for pow-wow. Some place where they just holds meetings.' That would be it then. Frowsty offices full of filing cabinets. Nothing interesting ever happened round here. Dead boring! They turned away in disgust.

♦ ♦ ♦

The first prisoners of war were a ramshackle bunch of ordinary Italian soldiers whose soft, brown eyes and generally downcast and -trodden looks struck a chord in local hearts, being so much like those of conscripted local lads. It was as if a straight swap had been made of these mothers' sons for their own. They also raised morale, for in the contrast between them and the slick, brash American troops, the inevitable outcome of the war was writ large and clearer than in any propaganda broadcast. For some reason, they were seasoned with a few misfiled German privates who were of more military habits and it proved important to keep the Italians and the misplaced Germans apart, given that these doubtful former allies were also now enemies following the fall of Mussolini and they eyed each other cautiously in any encounters, unsure what now united and what divided them. For the Italians at least, the safety of a warm hut in Wales was far preferable to the hazards of the front and they cheerfully settled in as farmhands, roadworkers and reservoir-diggers or laughingly undertook the task of erecting the quite unnecessary barbed wire fences around the camp that were supposed to keep them in but had not been completed in time. A third of the manual labour force of the UK was now PoWs and without them the autumn harvest would have been impossible that year. In the London ministries, men in suits worried that such good relations might undermine civilian war-fever and patriotic vigour. It was good if the enemy could be seen as slavering monsters but, in the countryside, no dead bombing victims could be laid at their door and the stern Non-Fraternisation Law was regarded as merely another piece of irritating nonsense from Whitehall that got in the way of life, like gas mask regulations.

And then, one day in 1944, after a night time loud with revving trucks and shouts, slamming doors and honking horns, the camp was mysteriously empty again and the disturbed citizens rose blearily to the announcement that a special train would be coming in at the station. The news buzzed around the town. Authoritative in their bicycle clips, policemen were briefed to tell the public calmly, 'There is no cause for alarm,' while not knowing themselves just what it was they were not supposed to be alarmed about.

For the boys, there was no question of going to school that day. It was recognised that the announcement suspended normal life as firmly as the declaration of war had done and all the children were hanging over the picket fences around the station through the long morning, while their parents kept a weather eye open through house and shop windows. At midday, they trudged disappointedly home but after strengthening themselves at the family tables, almost all rushed back on duty to hear the first distant shriek of the train, as teasing as any wolf-whistle, and note the sudden presence of armed soldiers lining the platform. Billy and his mates wormed their way through the crowds to be closest to the fence.

'Betcha it's Ike.' General Eisenhower had come once to address the American troops from the back of a jeep but it was understood that he was rather busy in Europe at the moment so it could not be him.

'Monty then.' He was excluded on similar grounds.

'The Royal Family has bugger all to do.' But they wouldn't come just for the hell of it and, anyway, someone would have tarted up the station to make sure they never left their own world where everything was new or freshly painted.

The train rounded the bend with a final screech and pulled along the platform, slowing and stopping with reluctance and a sigh of steam. There was a pause like the silence after a bomb. Nobody moved or spoke and the engine throbbed rhythmically through the void and the black smoke. Then a door at the far end opened and a British officer stepped out, straightened and blew a whistle. Older members of the public flinched in memory of 'Over the top' in the last war and then more doors were flung open and more guards stepped out backwards with rifles in their hands. Another pause and then, through the steam and smoke, alien figures in black appeared. They detrained with fussy dignity, casually looked around and adjusted their gloves and high-peaked hats, taking their time as if on an inspection tour of their latest conquest. SS! The words hissed into the sound of the escaping steam. A poster confronted them and asked politely whether their journey was really necessary. Apparently, it was. Then other German troops, an allsorts of mixed navy, army and airforce, stepped down in their wake.

The SS did not look like broken prisoners of war as Bridgenders knew them from Italy. Uniforms were immaculate, sleek gabardine, and complete, not tricked out with random, civilian additions like those of the Italians. Badges of rank and cap visors gleamed in the soft sunlight with muted menace. Boots shone with the forced labour of a hundred <u>Untermenschen</u> and heels clicked with aggressive impatience on the paving stones. How dare they be kept waiting! Some sported red arm brassards with offensive swastikas that they must have concealed somewhere and just distributed and the blackness of their uniforms, now scattered through the ranks, the stark whiteness of their shirts, were like a claim to higher status and rank through the disdaining of mere colour, like the dinner jackets the nobs flaunted at fancy dos. Such things impressed against the will. Many of the women bystanders wore frocks of dowdily reworked old curtains and bedspreads, the men pullovers of many colours from repeatedly unpicked and reknitted fuzzy wool. The SS heads were held particularly high, chins arrogantly so as they stared back at the watchers with eyes of pitiless blue that seemed to be automatically assessing their low racial purity with sardonic amusement and contain a threatening whiff of euthanasia.

A hostile murmur rolled out along the crowd, a mixture of fear and hatred as at the sight of an approaching predator. Unlike the smiling Italians who had gone before, these men would win no hearts. Memories of dead and missing bubbled up. One old lady burst into tears. Another screamed frail abuse and spat, a surprisingly copious stream of spittle from such a dried-up old woman. This was it at last, the unmistakeable face of the enemy, like really meeting a bright red creature with cloven hooves and two horns after years of seeing jokey pictures of him in the comics. The steam engine let out a long, low hiss and shuddered. Still more men poured overwhelmingly from the carriages, piling kitbags, forming up in neat lines. There were getting on for two thousand of them.

A British sergeant approached one of the black-clad officers uncertainly and saluted smartly - returned with a crisp 'Heil Hitler' as the watchers gasped in disbelief.

'Flippin 'eck,' breathed Billy.

'I'm afraid no transport is available. You men will have to march to the camp and carry their own luggage. It's about a mile.'

The officer raised a sneering eyebrow and looked down his nose, replying in perfect English. 'According to the Geneva Convention under which we are held, sergeant, as officers we only take orders from those of equivalent rank. We will wait here either until transport can be organised or a senior officer can be fetched. Off you go. Hurry along now.'

The sergeant ground his teeth. It had been a long day and it wasn't finished yet. His feet hurt and a cup of tea in the guardhouse beckoned wistfully. 'Look. I don't know nothing about that. Either you march, mate, or you're not going anywhere even if we have to sit here on our fannies all bloody night.'

'Under the terms of the Geneva Convention, officers cannot be forced to work. Carrying luggage is work. While Other Ranks may carry their own bags, officers will not.'

'I'm not standing here arguing the toss. Carrying luggage is not work. If you don't want to carry your luggage we can just bloody well leave it here on the platform and you and your men can do without it. Up to you.'

Cheers from the crowd. 'You tell 'im boyo.' A situation had been engineered where neither could back down without publicly losing face and force could not be used in a place like this. They glared at each other like two armies across the Channel.

'Leave it here? Oh no you don't.' The station master had emerged from his office and strode up, overcoat flapping, and poked the German officer in the chest. He was a man of some girth. Stout was his drink and stout it had made him. 'Listen you. I'm not having my platform left like this. Get this bloody stuff out of here and do it in double quick time or there'll be trouble. Sergeant Wilson, what's the meaning of this?'

The SS officer looked down at the long, dark coat with its brass buttons, reminiscent of that of a general, the peaked cap with its double icing of gold braid. This must be true authority. He stiffened, saluted and heelclicked and shouted an order and the troops shouldered up their kitbags as the officers lifted their leather bags.

'Right! Now follow me to the camp and no more of this nonsense.' Sergeant Wilson led them off in style, as if the victory were his own doing, swinging his arms and with his fat, little bottom swaying from side to side in best military fashion. The crowd cheered as though at a major armed breakthrough at the front. And then, as they turned outside the forecourt, the SS officer shouted another order and his men began goose-stepping past the butcher's empty shop window and the shocked mannequins of Dorothy Perkins, their boots crashing down as if on the faces of the onlookers. This did not look like a broken military machine, more like an invading army. Another shouted order and they broke into fine, manly song that fitted the thudding of their boots.

'Wir fahren gegen Engeland...'

An old gaffer, leaning over his fence and sucking on his tobaccoless pipe, shouted. 'Not Engelland you daft lot. You're in bloody Wales, boyo.'

The crowd burst into puzzling laughter.

'And you'll soon wear out your bloody boots walking like that you stupid sods.'

More laughter. The singing faltered. As they marched on, the SS stared straight ahead towards the camp gate and a final victory while the other servicemen began to steal shy glances at the people lining the roads. Some of the girls looked all right but the fashion sense here was really odd. A few had even dyed their hair a horrible green or that weird shade of red and their hands were hennaed like Turkish brides. One had

even painted her face bright yellow as if she was pretending to be Chinese. They looked like a right bunch of savages. What the hell was that all about?

◆ ◆ ◆

Lieutenant Colonel Edwin Darling had seen it all before. A career officer, in the First World War, he had been taken prisoner himself – a kriegie as they were called - and swiftly escaped from a German PoW camp to calmly rejoin his unit on the front, brushing off captivity as lightly as a schoolboy would an hour's detention. He spoke fluent German and, in a career that spanned the world and thirty years' service, had been awarded a chestful of medals including the Military Cross. They had been good times and, as for all old soldiers, the longer he lived, the better they had been. He was tall and unostentatiously handsome – his favourite line was 'Don't be formal, call me Darling' - but, at 51, considered too old for active service in the D-Day extravaganza. Darling was a man whose sense of Britishness had been formed in the heat of empire and was therefore unaware of those features in its constitution that might have seemed a caricature at home. He was full of decency and duty and found the speeches of Churchill distastefully boastful rather than inspiring and more than a little childish, like those chamber pots they sold with Hitler's leering face on the bottom. The man was putting on altogether too much dog. And as for dogs, what was that nonsense about the bulldog breed? He knew something of dogs and had always thought bulldogs the most stupid of animals in that they were prepared to take on grossly superior bulls and got themselves badly mauled for their arrogance, not the best image to have chosen in wartime. It seemed to him that the British virtues of modesty and understatement were to be packed away underground for the duration of the fighting like the oil paintings of the National Gallery. Nevertheless, he complied uncomplainingly with his unglamorous new posting as commandant of

Bridgend camp, knowing that If he protested, they would only tell him, 'Don't you know there's a war on?' How he hated that self-righteous and condescending expression with its implied sense of martyrdom. But as head of PoW camp 198, what grudgingly impressed the Germans most about him was his monocle, the true sign of an upper-class officer. And Darling had long mastered the art of using the accessory to express emotion as efficiently as a cat its tail. It was twirled tetchily, dropped in distress and screwed into its socket in outrage. He was in every way the sort of officer you wanted to be sent to your pointless death by.

Having also cultivated the eye of an escapee, Darling did a preliminary tour of his new command and was appalled at what he found. He knew that the best chances for escape always came in the first few hours after capture, before depression set in and the men found themselves in an environment designed to forestall any such endeavour. Captivity would affect the men in different ways. Some would form fierce, little cliques, other retreat into total silence and solitude, like switched off machines, waiting for eventual release. He knew that the chances of definitive escape were virtually nil, yet he knew also that the men would try if for no other reason than to pass the time and have some immediate short-term goal in mind. Somewhere in the camp, they were working at it right now. And these prisoners were not just run-of-the-mill. Many of the SS were classified as category C, category black, the worst kind of committed Nazi. No guard would be as determined to keep them in as they were to get out. He noted the ramshackle gates and the absence of a warning wire. In the camp in which he had been held, it had been a low single wire, a metre or so inside the main fence and marked a line beyond which any venturing prisoner would be shot. The guards, knowing the inmates were starved of tobacco, had amused themselves by throwing down cigarettes inches beyond it, tempting them into a zone where they would be allowed to open fire without warning.

He returned to his dank office and stalked past the dozing clerk and slumped at his own desk, holding his head in his hands and emitting a low groan. Then he took a deep breath, sat up, shocked the orderly, Corporal Crookshank, out of his peaceful slumber by bellowing for tea, unscrewed the cap of his pen and began to write a long and damning report through gritted teeth, the nib of his pen biting deep into the paper. He would be at it for some time.

There was no doubt, he noted, that the camp was simply in the wrong place. Prisoners with extreme political beliefs should be kept in isolated camps far from civilisation, Scotland or Dartmoor, where there was little ground cover so that any Nazi escapees would stick out like white rabbits in the Black Forest. Since they might be motivated by the urge to sabotage local installations, they should be kept away from strategic resources such as were packed into this local area - the huge ammunition factory, railways, ports, mines, steel plants and airfields that were scattered all over the county like pearls before swine.

It was also built according to totally wrong principles with buildings around the edges and up to the fence, not grouped in the centre and with open countryside extending close up to the wire outside. There was no path to allow patrols beyond the perimeter, no illumination except for a few acetylene flares that seldom worked, no watchtowers, no buried seismographic microphones or huts raised off the ground to make tunnelling impossible. With nearly two thousand prisoners, the guardroom was severely undermanned and the quality of the troops was execrable. In his time, he had commanded men of all possible hues and religions, learned to rattle off standard orders in tongues of mountain, swamp and desert, but never had he seen so many gathered together as if to refute the suggestion that Man was made in the image of God. There was a time when you gave malefactors a choice between the glasshouse and colonial service, exporting your troubles in their old kitbags. Nowadays, the choice was jankers or PoW guard duty and the men under his command were confirmed skrimshankers, fag-puffing old lags, boozers and barrack-room lawyers with an MO's treasury of leaky piles, trick knees, dicky tickers, gammy legs and dodgy backs. Their proudest possessions were not military honours such as medals and stripes but the treasured medical certificates testifying to the official standing of their various disabilities and the vast range of duties for which they must be considered ineligible. The smell of human failure was borne on the wind, overwhelming all the other noxious exhalations from the camp. If it had been intended that these old lags should pass on their military experience to younger ranks, this had been reduced to age-old techniques of fiddling, swinging the lead and the felonious misdirection of military stores. Worse still, these men were unmotivated, glum as a wet Welsh weekend and too tired to get out of their own way. Well, they had better keep out of his.

'Crookshank! Where's that damned tea I asked for?'

No answer. He was probably asleep.

◆ ◆ ◆

Oberführer Hermann Wenke brushed imaginary dust from the sleeve of his SS uniform and looked at himself complacently in the mirror. He had already removed non-existent dandruff from the oakleaf clusters on his collar. Although he was the same height as 5ft 6in sergeant Wilson and just as dumpy, in his mind he was a 1.9 metre icon of muscular, blond Aryan manhood and his gestures suggested he could as easily brush Wilson off too as he had at the railway station. He was far outranked by other army officers, but army officers he considered a lesser breed and he had appointed himself Senior Camp Officer, representing all the prisoners and he relied on fellow SS-members to enforce what he thought of as orderly discipline.

'What is it that you want?' he asked pleasantly to the ghostly image of the British NCO dithering behind him.

'I'm here to inspect your quarters.'

'And exactly why do you seek to do so?' He turned and cocked his head.

Sergeant Wilson faltered. 'I don't really…Those are my orders so please stand aside.'

Wenke took a deep breath and inflated himself still further so that he completely blocked the narrow doorway to his private room. 'But under the terms of the Geneva Convention – surely -prisoners are to be protected from harassment including public curiosity. You will not, therefore, inspect my quarters without my permission or I shall formally complain to the Red Cross of inhumane treatment.' He paused and smiled as if to a child of slow understanding. 'You may now go.'

Wilson set his face in what he hoped was a British bulldog expression of determination. 'My orders are…' He suddenly became aware of two other, really tall, broad-shouldered figures, looming up on either side of him, felt their breath on his vulnerable neck, the heat from their bodies.

'I said you may go, sergeant.' Wenke leaned forward in quiet menace. 'So go away little man. Now!'

Wilson looked around, though mostly up, at the two giants who were staring down expressionlessly from the shadows, shrank still further and scuttled away to their barks of harsh laughter.

Wenke grinned up at his men who grinned back with fine, Aryan, unfilled teeth. 'You have to keep at them, dominate them, humiliate them, turn them into the prisoners here. We shall draw up a rota to keep harassing them. I have considered setting fire to the camp but I suspect the concrete construction would be resistant to such attack. We may save that for later.' In the course of the war he had learned that destruction was a positive thing to be enjoyed for its own sake, like the pleasure little boys took in breaking windows. The one enjoyable part of surrender would have been having the time to destroy all their own carefully-maintained equipment in an orgy of smashing and detonation. Alas, that had been denied him but he still had hopes.

'The first thing to do is to create our ghosts.'

'Ghosts?'

'Yes. Prisoners conceal themselves within the camp so that they are missed at roll call which triggers a general alarm. The Tommies spend days searching the countryside for them, wasting resources, disrupting traffic and then one morning they simply reappear from hiding at morning roll call without any explanation. Not only does it make the enemy very angry, they come to distrust their own accounting systems. Here, the war goes on. Now, who are our first ghosts going to be?' His little face lit up with delight. He had quite recovered his bounce.

◆ ◆ ◆

The minister wrinkled his nose at the stack of papers his private secretary was sliding into his intray. At 11.30 it was too late in the morning to embark on anything new before lunch. He should go to the prefabricated British Restaurant round the corner and eat for ninepence. There he could enjoy some gruel-fuelled solidarity with the workers, a Woolton pie – just one of a dozen forms of disguised suet and potato currently on offer - eaten off a cracked plate while grinning and making V-for Victory signs at the dinner ladies in their knotted headscarves and waving his cheap knife and fork like someone in a works canteen. He had dropped by for breakfast there once and been offered a toast sandwich, a scorched slice of stale brown between two slices of slightly fresher white. But surely he had earned the right to a decent meal? Rationing and endless queuing, after all, were only for those who could not afford to sidestep them by going to a proper restaurant, a place of table cloths and French vocabulary. The dining room in the House did you a good game pie and at least you were spared the smoke of cigarettes made from the sweepings of stable floors but the company was even more poisonous and you were a sitting duck for MPs who wanted to bend your ear with tedious business. The Savoy grill was the place for a slap-up feed. They had an astonishing chicken chasseur that reeked less of casserole dishes than of the well-seasoned fleshpots of Paris before the war. One of those gobbled down in the company of the plutocrats who were doing well out of the hostilities would do him very nicely but the bolshie bastards in his own party would talk.

He sighed. 'What's this then, Henderson? What's all this blasted bumf?'

'PoW stuff mainly, sir.' His new PA was a fresh, young, Oxbridge smoothiechops, somehow excused the draft, who cultivated an irritating worldweary languor but he was sure they would learn to rub along together well enough. He was feeling increasingly worldweary himself.

'PoWs? Ours or theirs?' He looked out through the big, high window. Outside, the festive barrage balloons over Whitehall were tugging playfully at their mooring hawsers and, in St. James's Park, the WACs would be in full blossom. He felt like the caged canary he had owned as a child.

'Ours. That is to say, theirs. What I mean is German prisoners held by us. The usual monthly returns, minister, plus an absolute stinker of a report from Island Farm PoW Camp where, it seems, the whole Western world stands in danger of collapse.' He popped his eyes and bit his nails like Mary Pickford.

'Island Farm? Where's that?'

The PA flicked through the papers. 'Hmm! Says Bridgend. Somewhere in Wales, I think, but don't ask me where Wales is.'

'I shan't. Not my constituency at least but what's their...beef?' He had been developing his American contacts or perhaps it was just that lunch was still on his mind.

Henderson turned a page and pouted. '"Lack of troops, lack of supplies, inadequate security. I want, I want, yadayadaya." Standard stuff.'

The minister growled. 'Send them the standard letter back, then.' He leaned back in his chair and made a little chapel with his fingers. 'You start with "Don't you know there's a war on?" Hit them with guilt first. Then you embrace them in the greater purpose of the common good. "Overwhelming numbers of Germans surrendering to our advancing armies, every available soldier needed for the front, everybody stretched to the limit, the need for one last sustained push". You know the drill by now.'

'Righty-ho. Though perhaps we'd better leave out the stretching and the last push bit, sir, after all one of the complaints is the blocked drains that apparently can't cope with all the sudden new input - or is it output? –Very confusing - from the Jerries, with or without a capital J. Shall I pop in a signed photo, the sad but wise one? We've got rather a lot left, I'm afraid and they're starting to go curly at the edges. But we did have a run on you as uplifted and visionary, holding a pen.'

The minister rose to leave, grabbed his common-man porkpie hat from the hatstand and clapped it on his head with a contempt for appearance that negated any charge of vanity. Henderson, he knew, lunched frugally on a sandwich shared with one of the giggling secretary girls from the War Office who was his secret departmental gossip hotline. Henderson would rise. He reached a decision. He, himself, would walk across the park to his own club where he could discreetly dine on pigeon pie and a couple of glasses of red. Of course, that meant crossing in front of that great poster urging 'Better to eat Pot Luck rather than Humble Pie'. Pigeons, it could be argued, were a pest so eating them was sustaining the bucolic economy and, with France liberated, they should be getting some new stock in the cellar any day now. The umbrella-twirling walk would be his own self-denying contribution to the war effort.

'Good God no. I've told you before, Henderson, only female constituents get those, not official correspondents. That one you sent to the Home Guard by mistake didn't go down too well. I was told they fixed it to the dartboard in the officers' mess. If they have blocked drains this time, Christ knows where my face could end up.' Welsh was it he'd said? Lamb, a nice rack of crusted chops not too rare, now that was an excellent idea. His own chops began salivating.

'I'll be back at two – two-ish.'

As the door closed behind him, Henderson reached for the phone and dialled.

'Susie? The old man's gone. Come over?'

Ten minutes later, a very pretty girl with rich auburn hair, tapped at the door and peered coyly round it, then giggled and ran across to perch on his knee. 'Darling!' She wore a thin cotton dress that swirled around her young body as she moved. A loving peck on the cheek and she swivelled and pushed the papers on the desktop aside with one arm to unfold a packet wrapped in greaseproof paper.

'I'm hungry. A surprise today.' She giggled again as he nuzzled at her neck.

'Mmmm.'

'Bully beef.'

He stopped nuzzling and pouted. 'It was bully beef yesterday and the day before.'

'Yes, darling. But yesterday it was bullybeef with mustard and today it's bullybeef with Mum's home-made apple chutney.'

Henderson brightened. 'Apple chutney?'

'Well...apple chutney made with potatoes but you can hardly tell the difference if you use your imagination a bit.'

He sighed. 'The bread's made out of potatoes. The chutney's made out of potatoes. Is there anything nowadays not made out of potatoes?'

She tore off a piece, popped it into his mouth and sealed it with a kiss. 'Don't knock potatoes. Just think of all the things a clever girl can do when she gets her hands on a nice pair of big King Edward's, darling. And think yourself lucky to have a minister who's such a perfect poppet and leaves us his office every day. My Special Ops colonel's an absolute beast, so demanding.'

Jealousy flared in Henderson's narrow chest. 'He doesn't..?'

She laughed. 'No. Nothing like that, silly. I don't think he has any sex life. But he's gone all broody recently. He sits at his desk all day playing with his pencil and looking like thunder and then starts shouting at everyone. You see, all his past ops involved his chaps going off and getting themselves killed in large numbers and now they just come back alive. He takes it as a sign that quality is slipping. You know,' she took a great man-sized bite out of her sandwich and snuggled up kittenishly on his lap, 'I really think this horrid war might finally be coming to an end.'

◆ ◆ ◆

'I tell you now, I ain't going back in the pen without a gun.' Sergeant Wilson sucked desperately on his soggy roll-up as if at his mother's breast. His hand still shook. 'Them SS bastards put the bloody wind up me and no mistake.'

The corporal looked up from his paper and made a sour face. 'The old man says no guns inside the compound. It'd be too easy for them to clonk you on the head and grab one.'

'They're driving me nuts. When they're not singing them bloody songs, they're looking at you and jeering. "Hallo Tommy! How's your wife Tommy? Did she run off with the Americans Tommy?" You know that flood in town the other month? I reckon that was them too. Our blokes found a tree trunk jammed across the sluices upriver that caused it and it was chopped down not blown over. There was a work party there a few days before. I reckon it was them what done it. It's them SS bastards behind everything. They're running the place, driving the others on. We should take them out and keep them in a separate jail.'

'Against the rules, sarge. Geneva Convention. Anyway, his nibs says we have to spread them out through the huts otherwise they get together on their own and start thinking too much.'

'Thinking? They <u>think</u> it's funny to keep us up at night and the lazy buggers do f-all, just like our own bloody officers, so they can catch up on sleep any time they like. And the sheep don't help.'

'What've the sheep got to do with it?'

Wilson threw his dog-end away and reached for his tobacco tin to make another. 'When you're on guard duty they creep up behind you and cough just like a man. I swear they've had a go at the bogs too, flushing all the time, so you can't hardly hear yourself think and I was up three times last night what with them throwing stones at the wire and triggering a general alarm.'

'Mmm? Now there's a nice bit of crackling I wouldn't mind getting up three times a night for.' He held up a blurry picture of the latest 'forces' favourite' and grinned through bad teeth. Since the outlawing of horse-racing and the conversion of race courses for the processing of prisoners, he had given up on the written word entirely and only took account of the pictures in the papers. The horses might have made their way into the food chain but he rather liked the idea that his sausage roll might contain a Derby winner.

Wilson chuntered on. 'You know they take it in turns to "oversleep" or "forget" to sign up on the sick roster, so the roll call never works and we have to do it all over again and the old man only gets to give 'em two days solitary for it otherwise it's Geneva Convention this and Geneva Convention that. And they just stand there looking at you with this smirk on their faces.'

'Phwoar! I'd let her put a smirk on my face any time and wipe it off again with her great...'

'Fuck it!' Wilson slammed his fists down on the table. The tin flew off and clanged against the wall. He was shaking with rage and humiliation. 'Let's go and get a pint.'

The corporal looked at the clock and laid down his paper with reluctance. 'They're not open yet, sarge, and we're still on duty.'

'Fuck it! By the time we get to the pub they'll be serving. Come on. I'm buying.'

'Bloody hell!' The corporal got to his feet, stunned, reeling. 'You buying? This must be that end of the world they were always on about in Sunday school.'

♦ ♦ ♦

CHAPTER TWO

In the final months of 1944, V2 rockets began to fall on British cities, singly at first and then in ever-thicker showers. The infernal machines travelled upwards to the fringes of space before plunging down at enormous speed to deliver their payload of a tonne of high explosive. This was partly self-defeating since the joint weight and speed buried the nose deep in the earth and so corralled and deadened the explosive force delivered. But the fear they caused was amplified by their complete silence, unlike the farting, coughing V1s that made passing motor bikes objects of terror – a soundless Grim Reaper as opposed to death's noisy mowing machine - so that the first their victims knew of them was the explosion itself. They were completely random and so seemed like an act of God, not government, and popular belief immediately began to busily invent reasons for their falling on number 37 and not number 38 of any particular street – a failure of patriotism, an excessive warmth shown towards American soldiers, a son doubtfully excused service and in a reserved occupation as a 'D-Day dodger'. The British authorities had absolutely no defence against them and so decided, vainly, to deny their very existence.

'This is the BBC Home Service. Here is the news and this is Alvar Lidell reading it. One person was killed and a small number were injured in an explosion in Norwich yesterday. A series of similar minor explosions across Great Britain in recent weeks are thought to have been caused by defective gas mains. A spokesman said a programme of testing and maintenance was already in hand and assured members of the public that there was no cause for alarm.'

Despite orders to the contrary, members of the public <u>were</u> alarmed by this new form of gambling with death that was staking their lives on the turn of a card, the spin of a wheel or – more accurately – the precise point at which a German technician took his finger off the ethanol pump in distant Peenemünde but they were not fooled. They referred to the V2s tartly as 'the flying gas pipes'.

♦ ♦ ♦

'You will have heard of our new secret weapon, the Vergeltungswaffen rockets now raining down on the rubble that is all that remains of London and Norwich,' said Wenke with grim relish, 'and causing panic amongst the few reeling inhabitants staggering through the smoking ruins.' Radio sets had been swiftly assembled by the numerous technicians in the camp and locked to the German propaganda stations around the clock. The Tommy guards avoided entering the huts as much as possible and would probably have turned a blind eye to the radios anyway – anything for a quiet life. The newsreaders of the Reich were reporting the new wonder weapon, the repelling of the Allied invasion of Europe with huge casualties inflicted and the Führer's approaching inevitable victory. Each hut had a hidden apparatus and enthusiastic listening was mandatory. Anyone not listening enthusiastically enough would be called to account by Oberführer Wenke and the other SS officers who stalked the camp with stout cudgels and had been gathered together for this speech.

'Given this new advance, it now becomes even more urgent that we return to the conflict. So, I have decided that we shall escape. There will be not one but two tunnels. The first will be from hut 9, the second from hut 16, these being closest to the wire. Work will begin immediately. For security reasons, they will be referred to as Bertha and Brünhilde.' He thought that added a nice sense of destiny. 'Shortly before my unfortunate capture, I read the report on the escape of the British prisoners from Stalag Luft III and they demonstrated certain ingenuities which we shall now adopt and use against them.'

Some of the men looked disappointed. Tunnels were hard work, dirty and unglamorous. No one had ever won a medal or got promoted by digging a tunnel. They were fundamentally lacking in panache. Most of the PoWs were young men in their twenties – fit as gym shoes - and, with the physical impertinence of youth, thought no glittering athletic feat too much for them. Leutnant Tischler who had worked on cradles for loading torpedoes and was keen on skiing had submitted elegant designs for a device like a chairlift that would move under its own power on the cables slung between the electricity pylons that straddled the camp, requiring only a leap up and down of some forty feet to gain access. He admitted that was a minor theoretical problem that remained to be solved but was confident it could be. Another athlete, an enthusiastic pole-vaulter, proposed to execute a dashing double jump over the twin perimeter wire fences and rapidly disappear into the countryside using spliced broom handles and offering generous instruction to anyone else who was prepared to make their maiden vault during an escape attempt in his company. Yet another had proposed a giant and romantic balloon, powered by hot air or the swamp gas emitted by the faulty latrines, that would wistfully lift the whole camp up and away so that they could drift peacefully across the sea to Ireland or back to Germany depending on the prevailing wind direction. A more cunning suggestion had been to wait until snow covered the ground and then have men wiggle away under the wire while holding a white sheet over their heads as a cloak of invisibility. Anyway, they were officers and felt that tunnels were too much like the manual labour that Other Ranks went off to do every morning on local farms and roadsides. Tunnels were in every sense beneath them.

'The hut 9 tunnel will be under the direction of Major Prior, hut 16 Oberleutnant Kleist. Each tunnelling team will work independently with myself co-ordinating. We are lucky to have members of the Reich's Todt Organisation who are qualified engineers of great experience who have already conducted surveys. The soil here is soft clay and ideal for tunnelling and estimates are that a forty-foot tunnel should take four months to construct using relay teams of three men. Work will commence immediately and be carried out around the clock. Heil Hitler!'

◆ ◆ ◆

Lieutenant Colonel Darling rubbed his hands briskly together, partly to show get-up-and-go, partly to warm them up. The hut was chilly. Unable to control anything else, he had cut down on the lavish and wasteful use of coal he had noted throughout the camp when he first arrived, arranging the issue of smaller shovels that would exploit the natural laziness of the troops. Surrounded as they were with coal mines and with piled truckloads of the stuff streaming past the main gate daily, it was hard to maintain the message that coal was in short supply. He had also formed an obsessive interest in the level of the swill bins – personally plumbing the fetid depths for wasted leeks and onion peelings. Having been taught since childhood to eat everything on his plate, he rejected nothing - fat, bone and the ever-growing element that was simply unidentifiable – it was all grist to his mill and he swallowed it down ruthlessly and with forced gratitude.

'So what have we got today, corporal, to start the week? And I would appreciate it, for the future, if you could manage to march in in proper order and salute, not shuffle in like a seaside landlady serving breakfast, flap a hand at me like a performing seal and yawn.'

'Sorry, sir.' He laid down the mug of tea and stiffened. 'None of us got much sleep last night what with the singing of the prisoners and such like goings-on.' He executed an improved but still limp salute like a man holding up a wet fish for inspection. 'The usual Jerries are here again, sir, with a list of complaints and at ten you have a bloke from the Crown Film Unit.'

Lieutenant Colonel Darling emitted a silent, internal scream but set his face in granitic impassivity. 'Oh, very well. Wheel them in.' He felt like a housemaster, coming up for retirement, irritated by the same silly, delinquent tricks of his pupils that he had seen a thousand times before, that he had practised himself when in their position, but that they still thought were new. At any moment, he would learn the German for, 'Let's get the beak in a wax by ragging him.'

Oberführer Wenke and two other officers, one from the airforce, the other the navy, stamped in and Heil Hitlered.

Darling looked unmoved. The Italians who had been in the camp before were an unlucky bunch of odds and sods. But these were not odds and sods. These were simply sods. An army chaplain once told him that, sometimes, good people did bad things but mostly it was bad people and that seemed to make sense. As a commanding officer, he knew soldiers as earthy creatures, sites for foot fungus, Delhi belly and the clap. Contrary to Churchill's assertions, he also knew that most armies were determinedly pacifist. That they should be prey to political ideology and weaselling abstract nouns, he found loathsome and unnatural. Despite what that gasbag Churchill claimed, experience had taught him that soldiers properly fought for survival, local loyalties and out of shame, not so much Queen and Country, as your mates in your unit. Real war was life spiced with death, terror, excitement and pain, yet in a prison camp it was all the petty disputes of small-minded domesticity.

He screwed his monocle into place and glared. 'You are aware that I do not respond to that gesture that is not a recognised military salute. Please sit down, gentlemen. What can I do for you today?'

He had been right. They sat, smirking like urchins who had been caught being naughty and hauled up. Soon they would be taking turns to poke each other and kick their feet against their chairs.

'According to the terms of the Geneva Convention under which we are held...'

'Yes, I know.' Wearily. 'Please spare us that infernal cant. You wish to complain in the strongest possible way about what exactly? Before you make a formal complaint to the Red Cross. We have this charade at least once a week. What is it now? The use of straw-filled mattresses instead of box springs? Insufficient rind on the bacon supplied in the mess hall? The failure to segregate prisoners according to the branch of the armed forces to which they belong? The fact that airforce officers are guarded by army troops and not fellow airmen? The quality of perfumed soap offered in the shop whose smell differs from that of the Aryan soap offered in non-Jewish department stores and possibly made of the fat of their former owners?' The embers of a quiet internal rage began to glow and crackle and heat rose up into his face.

Wenke tutted. 'Lieutenant Colonel, you seem tired and strained. Take your time', he smiled soothingly – irritatingly - and leaned back in his chair. 'We have all the time in the world, as I believe you have pointed out on several occasions.'

'Of course I am tired. As our forces advance swiftly across Europe, we now have over a million helpless German prisoners to look after, just like abandoned, squalling babies, just like yourselves.'

Wenke's smile disappeared and he returned to his mantra. 'According to the terms of the Geneva Convention under which we are held, we wish to complain in the strongest possible way at the absence of bedsheets for officers which is a violation of our right to humane treatment.'

Darling looked up, astonished. 'Bedsheets? You want bedsheets. Is that it? Linen? Egyptian cotton? Or perhaps silk? If of silk, would that be in black or red?' He ostentatiously made a note. 'Request duly noted and refused. Now get the hell out of my office.'

Wenke did not budge. 'Might I have that in writing? According to the terms of the Geneva Convention under which we are held, I have the right to bring to the attention of the Senior Officer of the Protecting Power any complaint concerning our condition. There is also the matter of the food.'

'Excuse me, Oberführer, I may be Senior Officer of the Detaining Power here but you are not the designated Senior Officer among the prisoners. I fail to see why it is you that is here at all.'

'The other officers – those from the army - are indisposed.'

Darling reached for a piece of paper and studied it. 'They do not appear on the sick list.'

Wenke smiled. 'Their complaints are minor but incapacitating. They saw no reason to cause inconvenience to hard-working fellow officers by making them official.'

'Then perhaps I should ask the MO to examine them and establish whether they are truly ill or not?'

'They are all afflicted by bad backs which offer no external symptoms to the medical examiner but nevertheless cause the sufferer extreme agony.' Wenke's own pained look showed his sympathy. 'If you would prefer, we could hold an election for Senior Officer after the fashion recommended in your de-Nazification programme booklet to encourage democratic practices. I should, of course, win any such election. Shall we return to the matter of the food? It may be that improper nutrition is a factor in the ill health of these officers. Perhaps different arrangements might lead to a swift improvement in their condition.'

'Different arrangements? In what way different?'

Wenke leaned forward and spread his hands to unfold his grand plan. 'At the moment, food is delivered to the camp and then distributed to us by your men. What I would suggest is that it be delivered directly to us and we will undertake all tasks concerning its preparation and distribution to prisoners thus relieving you of this complex obligation and freeing up your own men for other duties. On our part, it would give the men something useful to do and allow us to offer food more in keeping with German tastes at no extra cost to you – in fact quite the reverse. For example, I would suggest we henceforth bake our own bread which will be cheaper than buying loaves ready-made and greatly reduce waste.'

Darling was astonished. Waste? He pricked up his ears. There was a lot of bread ending up in the swill. On the face of it, it seemed a good idea. It would remove an endless source of friction and complaint and ease his shortage of manpower and tight budget. When people said they loved France, they often meant they liked French cuisine. No one had ever loved Germany for its cooking, it was something best left to the Germans themselves and if the prisoners were kept busy spudbashing, a task they refused to do for him, they were less likely to be up to mischief elsewhere. He was unaware that, as Wenke talked, the other two were busily looking around, scanning the walls for maps or any other information that might be useful.

He brightened but this was a negotiation. 'Might it be the case then that, if food allocations were in German hands, the annoying banging of cups and plates and shouting in the mess hall, at every meal, would cease?'

Wenke nodded. 'I think that might well be the case. We should have to try it to be certain, of course.'

'And what about the habit of your men of spitting at passing civilians as they march out on work detail?'

'I have never seen this happen but I think that it might be prevented. If it ever occurred, it would merely be the men flexing their singing muscles out of sheer habit. Also, I would suggest that we should take over the accounting cards for prisoner purchases from the canteen and shop and the distribution of Red Cross food parcels which must take up a considerable amount of your time. We have men with extensive accounting expertise and they could do it much more efficiently. I believe it is an example of what you term in your colonies "indirect rule". After our victory, we too shall probably allow such arrangements to stand in the nations we newly administer.' There was a pause and they looked at each other in unwilling consensus despite that last shot.

Darling worked his jaw as if tasting the proposal. 'Very well, then. We will try the new arrangement for one month, subject to review.' An afterthought. 'Swill bins, naturally, remain entirely under our own control.'

'Naturally.'

The three Heil Hitlered and sauntered out, guffawing as the door shut behind them. Wenke stamped his feet in triumph like Hitler looking at the Eiffel Tower. The British did not know how to command, they simply cajoled. He now had unlimited control of the Soyer stoves of the kitchen, his boots across the throats of any prisoner who might oppose him and could begin stockpiling food for the escapees to take with them without anyone noticing. Since they would be running the camp shop, they would be able to arrange some form of exchange of plastic camp money for British pounds through trade with the underfed Tommy guards. Even more usefully, the SS now controlled the raw materials for making the camp's illicit alcohol. They had become bootleggers, which gave them ultimate power over Other Ranks – though, naturally, such inferior forms of distraction and stimulation would only be permitted to non-SS men.

Back in his office, Darling breathed more easily, a weight lifted from his shoulders and the tightness in his chest dissipated. Outside, the clouds parted and sudden sunlight streamed into the room and bathed the tawdry, careworn furniture in a forgiving, honeyed glow. Perhaps this was the start of a new phase, the PoWs realising that it was in everyone's interests to co-operate. There was a noise and he looked up to see one of the Other Ranks prisoners waving cheerily from outside, busily washing the windows, polishing up the glass with an old pair of German army underpants – swords beaten into ploughshares - and considerable gusto. Perhaps it was an omen of better times to come.

The orderly knocked, did a passable impersonation of a real soldier marching and saluting for once, and ushered in the man from the Crown Film Unit. Civilian dress. Horn-rimmed, tortoiseshell glasses. Corduroy trousers. A floppy bow tie. Horsey teeth. Mid-forties. Tweedy jacket that people once called a 'ratcatcher'. Obvious shirt-lifter. Well, it took all sorts. In war you got used to rum things. He knew the unit as the source of those loathsome little films about 'Why We Are Fighting The War' or 'What's It all For?' that his bods had to yawn their way through as well as the more popular cinematic offerings about VD that elicited a more vigorous response with their lurid images of seeping and inflamed genitalia that some found worryingly pornographic and their embarrassed doctor who only remembered, in the nick of time, to point with his pen and not his finger.

'Bevington-Smythe,' he introduced himself with a pale, bony handshake and settled hat, scarf and bag about himself. All he needed to be complete was a cat curled on his knees. As he sat, the trousers rode up to reveal scraggy ankles and socks whose pattern seemed like a homage to Aztec exuberance. 'Wilfred Bevington-Smythe. Crown Film Unit.' He passed across a visiting card.

Darling bellowed for tea, strong, manly, overbrewed tea with lots of sugar. 'And exactly what can I do for the Crown Film Unit, Mr. Bevington-Smythe?' He set down the card. It bore the image of a film camera with arched eyebrows and a grin on its lens.

'Well, sir. It's like this. Now that the war is moving on to a new stage with millions of German civilians about to fall into Allied hands, H.M. Govt. takes the view that a top priority is the calming of the German civil population's concerns about the fate of their menfolk while forward planning make decisions about ultimate repatriation. Some very nasty rumours are being circulated about our running concentration camps and general mistreatment, which are seen as discouraging surrender and co-operation, so the time is ripe for some sort of a little film showing how rather nice we are actually being to our German guests. You can imagine the sort of thing – lots of handsome, young, blond chaps with their shirts off laughing and playing handball in the British sun, tucking into good British eggs and bacon etc. with nice, shiny, German teeth, pitchforking hay into barns - for the benefit of the folks back home.'

'It sounds rather like the Hitler Youth.'

'Exactly!' Bevington-Smythe beamed. 'Knew you'd understand. They'll need hardly any training at all. It would also please our American cousins who seem to want to completely deindustrialise Germany after the war and turn it into a copy of small-town, rural America. Hamburgers eating hamburgers, what?' Darling looked blank. 'Oh, you don't know what a hamburger is?' Bevington-Smythe pouted. Of course, this was the backwoods not sophisticated Elstree. 'Never mind. Anyway, your camp has been selected as a suitable candidate for shooting.' He lowered his eyes and his voice. 'The minister takes a particular personal interest in seeing this project through.'

'Really? I shouldn't have thought...I should have thought he had more important...and why's that pray?'

Corporal Crookshank entered, slopping mugs of tea, walking with bent knees like a man in an egg and spoon race, and set them down on the desk, saluted and retired. Bevington-Smythe cast a baleful glare down into the depths of the brown liquid and pushed his gently away. There were other rumours circulating about the military slaking tea with bromide to push the sexual damper in.

'Well, it may have something to with his being my uncle, but that's by the way.' He trilled with Tinkerbelle laughter. 'The important thing is to get your authorisation to do some shooting around the camp as soon as the weather clears up. Too gloomy at the moment. Bad visibility. Countryside looks a bit drab and maybe we could arrange for things to get a general lick of paint and scatter a few pots of marigolds around. The whole thing would be entirely for German consumption, of course, total embargo on using it here. What you might call a Kraut-pleaser, what? Uncle George is keen that people over here mustn't get the idea that PoW camps are places where the Jerries are having a jolly holiday because they get the same rations as our own troops while civvies are roughing it and living on bread and pullet. That would never do. Comparing prisoner and civilian diets is a can of worms. Uncle George would ship us both off to the Siberian salt mines, like as not.' He laughed his worrying laugh again.

Darling frowned at the sound. 'Well, there's the matter of getting the prisoners to co-operate. Not to be underestimated. God knows, they can be difficult, very difficult. Running a place like this calls for real negotiating skills.'

'Really? Oh hard cheese! Leave that to you, sir. But I should have thought it would be fairly straightforward in a nice, happy, homogenous, little camp like this. You should see some of the problems they're having where the Jerries are mixed up with <u>Untermenschen</u> from the occupied countries who volunteered to fight for the Nazis and are now beginning to think they jumped the wrong way. Anyway, don't underestimate what we can do in the cutting shed once it's in the can, chopping it all up and splicing bits together to tell our story of hope to a defeated nation. You'd be amazed how small changes in processing make a hell of a difference to the final result so that a couple of happy faces can be made to spice things up and stretch a looong way. Right then, I'll tell dear old Uncle George you're all for it, keen as mustard in fact?' Darling managed a wan smile. 'And we'll be in touch once we're issued with film stock. Supplies of stock are a bit tight at the moment. But, in a couple of months we may even stretch to colour.' He rolled his eyes, gathered up his bag and other accoutrements fussily and rose to leave, casting a final suspicious look down at the mug of tea. 'I hope my car's all right. Some of your PoWs seemed a bit over-forthcoming, if I may say so, shouting things through the wire. They seemed to think I was someone called Tommy and they claimed to know my wife rather well.'

◆ ◆ ◆

'I couldn't get much,' said Private Schulz, puffing on a cigarette and scratching at his groin. There was another epidemic of lice in the camp, Wenke noted. Soon they would all be marched off for delousing, a shower and dusting with DDT. Such large movements of men always offered escape opportunities. Further east, in German camps, Wenke had heard, delousing offered a more permanent solution to infestations while their Russian prisoners were so hungry that they regarded fresh lice as a valuable supplement to their diet.

'The man had a funny accent as though his mouth was full of plum stones and I had to keep moving about so they didn't notice me listening outside the window. Also my English not so good is when people talk fast and I was panting as you have to keep breathing on the glass if you want to get a good finish and no smears. The soap they give you is of poor quality. It is very rough on your hands and leaves...'

'But what did you hear?' snapped Oberführer Wenke. It was infuriating that it was only enlisted men who could clean windows. An officer would have had better English though have done a worse job on the glass.

'Well, he said he was from something called the Crown Service.'

'The English royal family? Though they are really German and well-disposed towards us. We shall probably keep them after the final victory. Good. And what did he want in the camp?'

'Well, it didn't sound friendly at all. He said he wanted to start shooting us. He wanted men to shoot and some Uncle George – could that be the king? - had said it was a good idea. He said he would come back when the weather was better for his shooting in the camp. He was very keen to start operations and have young healthy ones to shoot. He also said something about chopping people up in the cutting shed for processing and there being too many Germans under British rule already and something about working with the Russians in Siberia.'

Wenke paled. 'What else?'

Schulz hesitated. 'Well I couldn't get it all but he said something about the Germans would be made to eat each other – only the Germans – though the British had a very bad diet. The Americans particularly wanted people from Hamburg to eat each other. He did not say why but he thought it was very funny. He talked of stretching the material and needing stock for the process and wanting to use mustard.'

'Mustard? You mean mustard gas?'

'I don't know. All I heard was mustard like you put on food and of putting the finished stuff in cans - oh, and something about salt and old cheese.'

'Dismiss, Schulz.' Wenke sat, lit his own cigarette and puffed shakily, his thoughts running wild. It was as bad as he had guessed it would be but he felt a sneaky sense of admiration for the soft Brits who were finally getting some ancient Germanic backbone in them.

Within hours, the most terrible rumours were circulating around the camp. Schulz's intelligence had done the rounds, been hardened and amplified. The British were about to reveal themselves in their true colours. Some of the PoWs were to be sent to Russia. The rest they were planning to shoot as soon as there were no more British prisoners in German hands to arouse fears of retaliation. They were then to be processed into tinned meat that was to be fed to the unknowing German population in a terrible act of revenge recalling the most horrific myths of ancient Greece. This, Wenke supposed, was the price to be paid for having a government made up of public school boys who drew on the legends of the classical past, not a vision of the manly, epic, Germanic future, and any lingering incredulity was overcome by the things they had seen and done themselves in the vortex of hatred that was Eastern Europe. This, surely, had something to do with the commandant's obsession with the swill bins. And had the British not revealed themselves unwittingly in that list of forthcoming foods that had fallen into his hands from the quartermaster's office that included 'swedes'? It would all start as soon as the warmer weather came and mass movements were easier. In the face of this planned atrocity, the need for escape was now even more urgent.

♦ ♦ ♦

'A prison hut is like a college,' Horst declared in a strong Bavarian accent and prodding at the dirt with a sharpened chair leg. 'It brings together people from all sorts of backgrounds, exposes them to each other's different ways, extends their knowledge through new experiences and widens their vision.'

He pushed a bucket of mud blindly back along the squelching tunnel with his legs to Willy who chuckled at his infernal optimism and wiped the sweat from his eyes with the fragment of torn vest that still clung to his torso. It made no difference. Neither could see much of anything. They were working in almost complete darkness like earthworms in the glow of a tiny lamp powered by margarine. Horst was a sub-mariner, used to confined spaces. This was possibly easier than crawling into a torpedo tube and knowing that only a thin hatch lay between you and millions of litres of icy water outside this steel coffin, just waiting to crush and drown you, while someone tapped his finger laughingly on the button that would open it. That had been part of the hazing when he joined the crew of U-245. They had also bleached his hair with battery acid and put dead prawns in his underpants. Good times.

Horst had joined the navy at seventeen and gone at once for the new thing that was submarines. The war had been a hot and sweaty experience and stinking of chlorine but combat was like a shooting gallery at the Christmas fair with little sense of reality. Hit a tin silhouette and win a prize. It was only on land, with the sub pens cut off by the Allies and him a fish out of water, that he had really seen death at close quarters. Violence is not pulling a trigger or pressing a button to release a puff of compressed air. It is the wet and sticky impact of flesh on human flesh.

Willy was airforce, used to being able to see the far horizon with the wind in his hair, so less happy down here. Sometimes he would shake uncontrollably and have to rush back up to the hole for air, flopped over the rim of the tunnel mouth, panting it in with a noise like an angry donkey. Now his hand hurt with a throbbing pain. The palm had been badly burned, pulling back the flaming canopy of his plane – Perspex gave such a cheerful flame - and had shrunk and puckered as it healed. They said it would need surgery before he could hope to get back full use of it. He was shot down over Brest, which was where Otto, the third of their little group, had designed the bombproof submarine pens that housed Horst's vessel when it was in port. It all came around in the end, brothers in arms.

'Come out, Horst.' Otto's urgent whisper echoed along the tunnel to the other two. 'You've gone far enough. We need to put in more roof support and shore it all up. You're right under the pathway. You'd think they'd have the sense to drive the odd heavy truck around the camp to cave in any tunnels but if the guards put on any more weight, they'll crash through the path and just crush you with their fat arses.' Horst got the giggles. Willy could feel him quivering and got them too as they slithered backwards in a twin breech delivery. Soon all three were collapsed, naked and streaked with dirt and sweat round the tunnel opening, gasping and choking with suppressed laughter.

The tunnel began from a corner of one of the smaller rooms, tucked away under one of the bunks. The other tunnel was actually underneath a stove and a makeshift pipe of empty milk tins, joined together, allowed it to be moved and replaced while still alight so that guards never searched under it. The worst part had been getting through the concrete foundation, pecking at it with a sharpened bar from the window, with the men singing Beethoven's <u>An die Freude</u> right outside the window, over and over again.

Otto, of course, who was musical, had felt the need to tell them the original title of the Schiller poem it was based on had been <u>To Freedom</u> not <u>To Joy</u>, changed because of fear of the repressive authorities of the time, which made the whole thing more apt but had annoyed the SS when he pointed it out. But then, by freedom, poor, stupid Schiller had meant rule by Napoleon, another shortarsed dictator. Otto felt you had to look for the poetry of life and ignore the crap that the lunatics on both sides fired at you. But he was a survivor from a more sceptical age. Having been told all his life that it was the unbelievers, the doubters, the selfish that caused all the trouble in the world, he now saw clearly that it was quite the opposite. It was the faithful, the fanatics and the self-sacrificers for a greater cause that wreaked havoc in people's lives. Otto was the least nervous, older, married, someone who had seen plenty of thought oppression in his Christian schooling. It came naturally to the younger men to call him 'Uncle'. He was from Hamburg like Willy and just wanted to get home and see what the Allied bombing had done to his family before the Russians got there with their prodding bayonets. There had been no letter from them for months.

Whatever else it did, the tunnel was good therapy but Otto was glad when the choir switched to <u>Lili Marlene</u> which – he recalled - Goebbels had tried to ban earlier in the war. He forbore to point that out. You should only push the men in black so far. Otherwise, the camp's only regular relief from martial music was a single tinny recording of <u>Eine kleine Nachtmusik</u> played on a gramophone in Hut 25 every evening at lightsout with the window cast wide open to the world. The names of the principal performers had been carefully studied by the SS and declared racially pure. Otto would bide his time before revealing that one of them was playing a soaringly beautiful ancient instrument made by the Amati family who were Jewish.

'Do you believe all that stuff about the Tommies shooting us if we lose the war?' asked Willy, gloomily lighting a cigarette to soothe his panting lungs.

'Shhh!' Otto held a finger to his lips. 'If Wenke hears you even suggest we might lose, there'll be trouble and the men in black will beat you till your face matches their uniforms. He can't think beyond empty slogans, just like the priests who brought me up, long before all this started. You're too young to remember any of that. You can't even get baptised now until you are twenty whereas we had it rammed down our throats as tiny kids! Come to think of it, they used much the same methods. The war will never just be "over" for Wenke. The "final victory" will always still be just around the corner like Heaven for the Catholics. The problem with words is you sometimes know whose mouth they have been in before yours.'

'All right, then. Let's put it this way.' Willy took a deep breath. 'Do you think the Tommies really plan to shoot us all after our inevitable, final victory has come and they occupy the Fatherland and there are no longer any Allied prisoners in our hands to use as hostages?'

They began sniggering again and Horst burst out in open, full-throated laughter. 'Who the hell knows? You remember how they told us that every city in England had been totally destroyed by the Luftwaffe and how astonished we were when we came here and saw them still standing? But, seriously, we can't just sit on our backsides. We have to get out before it's too late. I can feel our youth shrivelling on the vine.' He clutched his balls melodramatically and groaned. 'Well, not yours Otto. Your fruit is already shrivelled with only the pips left.'

'Not too shrivelled for a Sonderspätauslese, a final autumnal pressing, the sweetest and finest wine of all.' He grinned. 'Or so ladies say.'

Horst tapped him on the arm. 'By the way, you used the word "Austria" the other day. No one noticed but don't do that again. It's the Ostmark of the Reich now.'

Willy was unconvinced. 'But if they don't plan to shoot us, like Wenke says, why are the Other Ranks setting up wooden poles all over the camp? Who are they going to tie to them if not us?'

Otto polished his smeared glasses, exasperated. 'I've seen one of them completed, over the far side. They're to hold loudspeakers. They're going to bombard us with propaganda about the war and drown out the singing.' He couldn't resist adding. 'Of course, they could also contain microphones to hear what <u>we</u> are saying.' He grabbed what looked like a rattling bundle of firewood. 'Anyway, I'd better get down there before the next shift turns up or we won't achieve our quota and Wenke will be on our tails again with his, "We must achieve two metres a day for the Führer". Sooner or later I will tell him Roehm wasn't killed – I mean Rome wasn't built - in a day.'

They watched him squeeze down and disappear with a groan - it was an eighteen-foot vertical drop to the bottom and the start of the tunnel proper - so skinny and old-looking compared to them. He wasn't really a soldier at all. It was just that anyone who worked for the Todt Organisation that handled the Reich's building projects was conscripted and given a joke army rank so it was easier to shoot them if the project turned bad. The Nazis had finally solved the problem of unreliable tradesmen that was the curse of the middle classes.

Otto was really just a middle-aged civilian who shouldn't be here at all and his last job had been redesigning the army goulash-cannon, the mobile field kitchen, for installation in railway carriages. Was it possible that one day they would look like that? The mind said yes, the heart said no. They would go and wash and then play handball out in the yard and do push-ups for Wenke to see and nod his head at. It was important not to leave traces of dirt around, though they had intimidated the guards so thoroughly that they almost never came inside the huts any more. The bucket of mud they had filled would have to be passed through the window and dumped on the garden. 'We must cultivate our garden,' as Uncle Otto always said but they never knew why.

They had petitioned the commandant to allow them to enlarge it to grow more of their own food and the booby had been so pleased they almost felt sorry for him. He never seemed to wonder why they were always just digging in bare earth, digging, digging, digging – "digging for victory" as the Tommies said.

'That film,' Willy said quietly, worry etched into his young face. 'The one they made us watch about the concentration camp and the Jews. Was that real?' They had been marched into the hall and seen the projector all set up and expected something with Bing Crosby – der Bingle – or Charlie Chaplin. But no, it was just jerky, fuzzy, badly-edited footage of a weird world, bounded by barbed wire like their own, but with silent, alien faces – barely human – just peering out at them in eerie, black and white emptiness. Then some German-speaking officer had come and ranted at them about war-crimes.

Horst clapped him on the shoulder and shook his head, laughing. 'Look, it was from the Soviets. You saw their uniforms everywhere, right? They filmed it. They set it up. Do you think you can trust them to tell the truth? Wenke said what it really
showed was how the Jewish-Bolsheviks treated German-speakers the wrong side of the border and they had just changed all the signs around for propaganda purposes.

He should know. Relax. Don't believe a word of it.' He slapped him on the shoulder with a grin. 'Sometimes, Willy, you are so gullible.'

♦ ♦ ♦

CHAPTER THREE

'If you'll take my advice, old man, you'll get yourself some Poles. I've been round quite a few of the camps and they make all the difference between the sort of problems you're having here and a nice tight camp.'

Lieutenant Colonel Darling did not like this greasy, little man from Security Services. He had flashed an identity card with no name – 'If it had a name it wouldn't be secure would it?' - but did he hold military rank? Surely not. But everything about him rankled. Surely, no other man in England had a Hitler moustache and the collar of his mac, with its missing buttons, was filthy, shiny with old hair cream, and looked like a dandruff farm. He also had a Middlesex whine. Darling hated a Middlesex whine even more than a phlegmy Glasgow bark.

'Some poles?' He snorted plummily. 'What the hell would I do with more poles? We've got them set up all over the camp already for the promised loudspeakers which still haven't come. And what do you know about our difficulties?'

'Not poles. Poles!' He snickered through nicotine-yellow teeth. 'The chaps from Poland, our brave allies with a capital P. After what the Jerries did to them out East, they don't bother too much about the Geneva Convention, if you get my drift. Polish guards welcome the chance to enforce a bit of physical discipline with a good firm hand which is what's needed in the camps. It's all about sticks and carrots and Poles are definitely good with sticks. They'll make great lion tamers after the war. As for the other thing, we're paid to know what's going on.' He tapped the side of his nose and winked horribly. '– apart from all the billy-dos you keep writing to the ministry detailing your woes.'

'You read those?' Like most soldiers, he had a deep contempt for military administrative staff and a still-deeper one for civil servants.

The man pulled out a packet of cheap woodbines and lit one without asking permission or offering. Darling pushed the ashtray at him in silent rebuke but he just lobbed the spent match into it with the sort of gesture young louts practise to be considered stylish and continued unabashed. 'I think we're the only ones who do. We read everything, old man, including the letters your inmates write back home. Some of those contain quite a lot of info about you. You might be surprised - some of the things they say. Bet your ears are red. I know our censor girls' cheeks are. By the way, how come you haven't planted any informers among them? Standard drill I should have thought in a camp of this kind. Think Poles again. Some of them can even pass for German and so a scattering through the camp works wonders. Usually barbers are the best, get everywhere, hear everything, a pair of scissors makes a man invisible but I don't see any sign of that in your memos. Bad oversight if I may say so. Stool-pigeons are good at ferreting things out.' He did not seem bothered by such mixed zoology but picked at a strand of loose tobacco on his tongue and attached it to the side of the ashtray with wet saliva and wandered into...'Oh, and a word to the wise. The coves at the ministry are very literal-minded. For God's sake stop going on about 'taking concrete steps' or they will send someone round to knock out the hut doorsteps. And duckboards. Those raised duckboards you've laid around the perimeter. Not good. It means they can hear the sentries clumping up from a mile away and makes it easier for passers-by to chuck stuff over the wire undetected.'

Darling bridled. 'Who would want to...?'

'Fifth columnists!'

Darling frowned. '<u>Are</u> there any fifth columnists? I don't think we even have any third or fourth columnists around here. Surely, they've all given up by now – if there ever were any in the first place. Anyway, we don't have a problem with stuff coming in. It's the stuff going out. The prisoners throw paper darts out and our orders are to hunt them down and give them to the translators to check for any information useful to the enemy.'

'Be alert! Britain needs more lerts, haha! That's why planted informants are so useful. Use the pillow-biters.'

'The what?'

'The Germans have other names, some of them quite creative - "banana-peelers", "spinach-researchers". I rather like "gherkin-eaters".' He raised an eyebrow. Darling looked simply bewildered. He sighed. 'You're an old public school man aren't you? Prisoner yourself in the last war? There you are then. You'll know how all about it from both ends, as it were.' A slight sneer curled the corner of his lips. 'Grammar school boy myself. But two thousand fit, thrusting, young chaps crowded together, rubbing against each other the whole time, half-naked and bored to death, literally a hotbed for a touch of the other. They're all at it just, getting stuck in, like our blokes in the Jerry camps. Stands to reason. You won't find that in the official reports of course but some of the military prisoners are still seeing action every night.'

Darling blushed red and looked as if his own bottom had been pinched. 'I assure you that nothing of that kind has ever...'

'Oh come off it. Drop your corsets. Young men's grief or happiness lives in their trousers and reading 19th century novels just won't do it for them. Look, the SS are a bunch of peacocks and have this virile manliness obsession with nice shiny uniforms and muscles and would never admit to bending down in the shower to do more than pick up the soap, so you use that to split their loyalties. You start by checking on the theatricals in your camp, the pretty ones that play the female parts on stage, and say you'll post a notice about the forbidding of the observed, rampant, unnatural activities in the camp that dishonour the name of the German army and it will suggest that this started in the theatre groups. The SS would go crazy and use them as scapegoats and they know it. More than their lives would be worth. So, to avoid that, they become your informants and, of course, many of them really <u>are</u> carrying on with senior officers so they have access to the parts others can't reach.'

'But doesn't that expose them to fearful risk?'

He shrugged and puffed smoke. 'If the shit hits the fan and you get there in time, you pull them out and offer special protection. We have some rather nice little forestry projects where they can all go camping together and read poems to each other and the squirrels in the early dawn mist. If not, the SS usually string them up to scare the others but they make it look like suicide by the over-sensitive so it's off the books and still doesn't spoil your neat, official records.' He breathed complacent smoke.

Darling looked huffy. 'I should regard all that as a rather unpleasant thing to do, I'm afraid.'

'We're dealing with some rather unpleasant people in case you hadn't noticed.' There was a sharpness in his voice. I suggest you think again...' There was a taut silence. Darling glared back, clearly thinking many things. There was something in this man's eye that suggested he was about to say...He hoped he would not say it. He knew he was going to say it. Finally, he said it. 'Don't you know there's a war on? And it's a funny war. The blokes who shed most of their blood for the war effort are the conchies. You should see them lining up outside the transfusion centres giving pints of it! Great bleeders, the conchies. But that's not why I'm here. Something rather more serious. It's this business of sending Christmas cards to the Führer.'

'What? But I haven't been...Oh, I see, you mean the prisoners. Have they? Can they? No one told me.' Christmas. There would be nothing in the shops and in the age-old, mythical battle between light and dark, darkness wrapped in blackout drapery had clearly won.

'Exactly my point you see. An informer would have tipped you off and a few decent Poles would have whacked that on the head right away and snapped their pencils. But there's a bigger problem. Let me tell you a story, absolutely hush-hush of course.' He looked around, wide-eyed, to stress the hush-hushedness of it. 'We have an informer in PoW Camp 23, Devizes, Wiltshire. Now he's a solid chap and we've checked his gen pretty thoroughly and we can be sure it's absolutely kosher. We have uncovered a serious plot that represents a grave threat to national security.' He let that sink in. No drum roll but how often in life did you get to deliver a line like that with a completely straight face? 'The plan is for a hardened core of their commando officers to escape from Devizes on Christmas Eve during a loud version of 'Silent Night' that will serve to hide their absence. They will take over the nearby army base, pared to a skeleton staff for Christmas, loot the weapons and return to free all 7,000 inmates and arm them for immediate combat. I should add that the armament includes the latest Sherman tanks used for training purposes on Salisbury Plain. They have also discovered the locations of nearby fuel depots, airfields and food stores and the plan is to take those over and then move against all the other PoW camps grouped in the area and begin a systematic insurgency while the country's defences have been pared to the bone for the invasion of Europe. They will be augmented by a team of crack paratroopers dropped onto the Plain, disguised as Americans, who will lend necessary backbone and further confuse our own defences. Their ultimate goal is an attack on London itself. Bletchley have been independently picking up messages about training fluent English-speakers for a special mission of exactly this kind. Now that we know their plans, they will, of course, be stopped in their tracks and we'll haul off the ringleaders to cool their heels somewhere nasty. The thing is the Christmas cards.'

'What have Christmas cards got to do with it?'

'There is a campaign to annoy us by sending cards to Adolf and it started in Devizes but somehow almost every other PoW camp is now part of it. Spreading like the clap. They're all scribbling away at their holly and robins like kids in primary school. We tried to put the kybosh on it - 'bringing unreasonable comfort to the enemy' and such - but the Red Cross won't have it so we have to let it run and our hope is that the cards will gum up what's left of the German postal service as efficiently as enemy turds do your drains. Oh, yes, I've read the memo. Either way, Adolf's mantlepiece is going to be pretty full this year. But the point is, it shows the camps are communicating with each other. They're somehow in contact, including yours, and we don't know how. It could be a concealed radio or coded messages written home or something in food packages. Therefore, we have to assume yours is part of the greater conspiracy too.'

'So what would you have me do, take their crayons away?'

'We are aiming to nip it in the bud, of course, and the Yanks have been tipped off to take extra precautions but we want to let things run for a bit to find out as much as we can about the ringleaders. Now, it's just possible they may try to bring things forward, or that the conspirators here may not hear in time that we've taken care of business in Devizes, so you should be twice as vigilant. Double the guards. Oh, and watch out for them singing Silent Night. There's a lot of that goes on around escape attempts. Sense of irony perhaps. Once the Jerries get an idea in their heads they tend to stick to it. But above all, old man...'He laid a finger melodramatically on his lips...'Remember, be like Dad: Keep Mum.'

♦ ♦ ♦

'It's the dirt. It's changed colour, not black any more but bright yellow clay. We can't just spread it out on the garden like we used to. It stands out like a coloured dog. Even our guards would notice. What should we do?' Willy was perplexed and, as always when perplexed, he asked Uncle Otto what to do.

'Clay? Perhaps we should start pottery classes.' Otto grinned at his own bad joke but the others just stared back blankly and he wiped the smile off his face. He slapped his knee. 'Actually, that's not a bad idea except for the difficulty of getting fuel for the firing. Maybe sculpture classes.' In one leap of the imagination he could see it all.

The camp was full of men with academic qualifications that they used to start courses of instruction. It was not unusual to come across a roomful of battle-hardened men writing essays in English on 'What I did in my holidays' and laughing earnestly at the studied absurdities of Oscar Wilde or thrilling to the omniscience of Sherlock Holmes – though instructors had to cope with many alleged cases of 'the rats ate my homework'. There were law and history graduates, men out of agricultural college, the odd Todt engineer like Otto. Why not potters? They could get in a small, official supply of clay through the Red Cross for therapeutic rehabilitation of injured soldiers – Willy's hand! - and then pad it out outrageously with stuff from the tunnels.

Whether they knew it or not, Otto saw that what wore the men down more than anything else was the total absence of any form of beauty in their tight little world of rain-soaked concrete and rusty wire. It was so easy to forget that this grey life was better than death. Sun-dried clay was a recognised modelling material, if the sun ever shone in this God-forsaken country. Of course, the men would all end up modelling their own busts of big women's busts but it would keep their sticky, little fingers busy. He looked through the window where rain hissed on the glass, filthy, unlike those overpolished windows in the administrative block. Horst was almost right. A British PoW camp was not quite a college, more an alma martyr, it was to be understood in terms of the bleak, arbitrary authority and pointless rules of one of those terrible public schools the British so prided themselves on.

The camp commandant, he knew, would go for it. He loved to see his charges beavering away at something creative. Perhaps a monocle favoured a narrow, half-blind view of reality. There had been that pig-breeding project out on one of the farms, feeding them with swill from the camp, that was accounted a great success with lots of English jokes about 'bringing home the bacon' that didn't work in

German where you 'bring home the bread rolls'. An initial problem had arisen when it appeared that the local farmer stubbornly wanted to give all the pigs the names of Nazi leaders, pointing out that his own pampered bulldog was called Winston with no disrespect intended or felt. That caused a rumpus but, after much discussion and stamping of SS feet, all sides had reached a fair compromise and renamed the herd after figures from the Vichy French whom the Germans sneered at as much as the Allies and they had all felt genuinely sad when Marshal Pétain developed worms and had to be put down.

There had been other misunderstandings. It was inevitable, as the greasy man from Security had observed, that the absence of women had led to the embracing of the usual sexual outlets available in an all-male institution despite the official disapproval of the SS, so that there had been linguistic and cultural confusion over the English expression 'animal husbandry' but that, too, had eventually been cleared up - though with a few red faces and cleared throats. A request to make pots might just work if he could come up with a few well-turned justificatory phrases and "howl with the wolves".

◆ ◆ ◆

'I'll 'ave you son. I'll 'ave you - guts for garters, tits for tea and balls for breakfaaast.' Sergeant Wilson snarled up at the young soldier, foam at the corners of his mouth, eyes two insane, bloodshot, rolling marbles. A pair of corporals tittered from behind him. 'What's all this hoity-toity crap in your report?' He waved a piece of paper in the boy's face. '"Guardroom in unfit military condition. Discrepancies in ammunition log. Infringement of regulations involving segregation of prisoners and guards. Evidence of sentries drunk on station. Absence of duty sergeant for long periods while officially in charge". Since when does a snotty-nosed recruit like you get to write a report to the CO on me, Private Morris? Just because you matriculated. Lucky the old man's too busy writing his own reports to read anyone else's. If the duty corp hadn't picked this up and pulled it, we'd all be in the shit, your shit. Let me tell you what's going to happen, sunshine. You're just here awaiting reassignment to a front-line regiment but you ain't gonna make it. You'll find it's more dangerous here under good ole' Sergeant Wilson than on the Rhine facing the Krauts. You're going to wish you'd never been born is what.' He grabbed the boy's collar and yanked it down. 'Improperly dressed.' He leaned forward and cupped an ear to imagined speech. 'What's that you say? "The CO is a cunt?" Did you really say that in front of two other witnesses? That was stupid of you, son.

Right, well that's gross insubordination. Write that down.' He grabbed a beer bottle from the table and sloshed it down the boy's front. 'Is that drink I smell on you, boy?' He shook his head. 'Can't be 'aving that, can we? A sloppy bugger like you turning up in this condition for duty in front of bunch of foreign bastards. I'm putting you on a charge, son. I'm shocked, deeply shocked. You're a bloody disgrace to the British Army. What are you with your matriculation?

'I'm a bloody disgrace to the British Army, sarge.'

'Too bloody right you are.'

◆ ◆ ◆

The tunnel was taking longer than expected. Even with teams digging around the clock, progress was slow and that increased the risk of discovery. First, there had been a problem with the air. The length of time a man could stay down there digging got shorter and shorter as the tunnel advanced so they had rigged up a great snake of old Klim milk cans, top and bottom removed and stuck together and pumped air through it using a hand-turned windmill that a punkawallah turned between his legs. A favourite joke was for the operator to blow his farts into it under pretence of 'testing' and listen for the cry of outrage from the rockface below. Then, it was so dark down there, a rudimentary electric lighting system had had to be rigged up that tapped into the main power cable and kept working even after lights out. The problem had been getting their hands on some wiring but they had managed to steal a whole roll from the loudspeaker project. Astonishingly, no checks were ever made on materials and tools inside the camp to see if any went missing. Most recently, there had been the Great Sewer Pipe Catastrophe when the great, ceramic drain – up till then simply slightly disturbed by the undermining - had completely collapsed, flooding the excavations in sprudelling, reeking filth. Two men had narrowly escaped the nastiest form of drowning imaginable and the pipe had been hastily rebodged with the sort of sailor's emergency bandage used to block a ship's leaking hull. Ever since, the rancid toilets had only flushed grudgingly.

And now, with all the recent rain, the clay was still malleable, but horribly sticky. It was like spooning out soft toffee that stank of sewage with a teaspoon and it got everywhere, in your hair, your ears. Sooner or later, it would give the game away. You couldn't even just tip it out of a bucket of the stuff any more. More laborious spooning. Otto looked around. In one corner, there was a sort of alcove formed by the junction of two bare walls, a rare relief from the obsessive square boxiness of the buildings. The architect must have come back drunk from lunch to permit himself such whimsy in a construction otherwise totally devoid of any consideration of comfort or pleasure.

He pointed. 'There! We build a fake wall in a line straight across and store the clay behind it. There are some matching spare bricks stacked outside the mess-hall we can use. We smuggle them in, one by one. We can run up a wall in a couple of nights as long as we get lucky and there are no inspections. We can do the same in the other hut.'

Wenke had approved. He disliked Otto heartily but had to admit his usefulness. For the moment he would be tolerated but his time would come.

Willy and Horst made faces. 'Yeah but how do we manage without cement? We've got the bricks but you can't build a wall without mortar – stands to reason.'

Otto laughed. 'That's not quite what it says in the Bible but it's already been taken care of. We've got all the mortar we need.'

The most senior army officers had taken to themselves the luxurious privilege of having breakfast served every morning in their own quarters by their batmen. Henceforth, following a visit by Wenke, they suddenly disdained some of the enviable dainties they had previously enjoyed and developed a bottomless appetite for very thick porridge, enough for half a regiment, humped across from the kitchens – now under German control - by an orderly in a great slopping bucket and, despite advanced age and fastidious tastes, they somehow never left a drop uneaten. This change had not been stomached without protest on their side. Oberführer Wenke, something of an expert in the administration of castor-oil diets, noted with quiet menace that their guts would complain less at this imposition than their mouths did. The excess porridge neatly cemented the bricks together, thus making flesh countless generations of subaltern humour concerning its quality.

The change did not go entirely unnoticed. Following new orders, the contents of the buckets were ruthlessly checked for concealed objects. Nothing was ever found.

'Bloody hell! No wonder the bloody drains is blocked what with the way them greedy buggers is shovelling this stuff down,' observed one of the astonished guards, poking deep with a bayonet at the resisting lumps. But no further suspicions were aroused. They even christened the cheery, blond porridge orderly 'Goldilocks'.

When the matter came to Darling's personal attention, he immediately assumed that the object of the exercise could only be to smuggle in buckets to avoid his regulations concerning swill bins. He ordered them to be counted and numbered with paint and ticked off as they came and went in and out. Still nothing.

♦ ♦ ♦

CHAPTER FOUR

'This is the BBC Home Service. Here is the news and this is Alvar Lidell reading it. Reports are coming in of fierce fighting in the Ardennes Forest area of Eastern Belgium with large movements of German armour, infantry and paratroopers throughout the region. Allied forces have successfully repelled heavy attacks and secured their positions and taken large numbers of prisoners, some disguised as American soldiers. A spokesman said...'

♦ ♦ ♦

So the paratroopers had not been for a British plot after all but for a last desperate German counteroffensive that would be known in the West as the Battle of the Bulge. Oberführer Wenke had no doubt of its complete success – the British were lying about the outcome as usual, of course. At night he lay in his narrow bunk and dreamed himself among the cutout Ardennes trees with a low, icy fog hiding him and his men as they advanced like ghosts across the snow and picked their way through the conifers, dressed in white battledress, and gunned down the fat and complacent Americans as they chewed gum like cows their cud. The soft thud of the grenades was music to his ears, cushioned by the friendly snowfall, the smell of pine essence and fresh-spilled blood. He missed the kick of a recoiling rifle against his shoulder, the thrill of the hunter with his prey in his sights, the sharp intake of breath as it toppled. The light of the winter forest had a magical quality, the blue tones exaggerated like in an operating theatre, offering a unique sharp precision to the sniper. His breathing was slow and steady, each exhalation a slow pull on a trigger. The war had brought him the only excitement, power and purpose he had ever known and he hugged it severely like a child its teddy bear. In civilian life, he had been bullied at school, left without qualifications despite allegedly high intelligence and – driven by an aggressive father - become an inoffensive greengrocer with a particular knack for neatly wrapping awkward aubergines in quality newspaper for the middle-class shoppers of Berlin. He could still not look at a cosh without thinking of one. Then, one day, he had stood in the shop doorway and seen brownshirts beating up the rival local fruiterer - a big, intimidating man who habitually sneered at him and had communist leanings – joyfully hurling pineapples through his shop windows like hand grenades and he had wanted some of that. His military career had been propelled more by unfulfilled promise than solid achievement and had come to a rather ignominious end when, armed with only a pistol, he had found himself face-to-face - actually pinned to a wall - by the snout of an American tank, the kind they called Zippos because, being cheap and petrol-fuelled, they readily exploded in flame. Physically unable to move, he had raised his hands and dropped his weapon and regretted too late that he had not shot himself when the hatch clanged open and he saw that he had surrendered to grinning black troops as if from a Berlin cabaret.

 He drove the image from his memory and then, suddenly, the scene changed and he was back on the Eastern front in a hell of starvation and frostbite with the soldiers eating their horses as they themselves were hunted down and shot or dragged alive and screaming behind Russian tanks stuffed with whooping communists. A terrible cold invaded his legs and crept ever upward. He knew when it reached his head he would die of frostbite as so many in his unit had yet he woke in crepuscular gloom to find himself absurdly covered in sweat. In the morning, his hands were shaking as he lit a first cigarette, enjoying the heat more than the flavour, and stood on the threshold of hut 9, tracing the course of the hidden tunnel with his eyes and raising them to look out over the soft, smug Welsh countryside that he would soon be travelling through on his way back to the front like a lone arctic wolf. On his travels, he would see Britain's damp basement, Ireland, through a friendly porthole or was it a starboardhole? Even capture would be different here. Unlike the Americans and the Russians, the British were excellent sportsmen. Practice had taught them how to lose very well. By now, they were used to it. They excelled at it. But no, he could not go on the run himself.' He stubbed out that hope. His rank forbade it. But he would have the extreme pleasure of staying and witnessing the Tommies' discomfort. Perhaps the Führer would acknowledge his achievements by making him Governor of Wales after the final victory. He was, after all, a man of high moral principle. Wenke boasted that he had never raped a married woman and only ever shot civilians if he suspected they might sympathise with partisans but there was no road that could possibly lead back to greengrocery.

 Things were proceeding on schedule, "all in butter", with the tunnel projects and he passed them in review in his mind. Tunnelling quotas were being achieved thanks to the Todt man's installation of new sledges on rails to convey excavated dirt back more swiftly and efficiently to the tunnel mouth. A physical check had confirmed that they were nearing the wire, a man being sent to the end of the excavation to poke up a narrow tube through which he blew cigarette smoke. It was right on target like a V-weapon. The brilliant false wall had been successfully completed so the generals could go back to their belching, less costive, breakfasts to the relief of their guts and the por ridge-hauler's shoulders and the men had constructed a fake ventilation hole at the top of the wall through which they could push in balls of wet clay moulded with their hands. It fell with a satisfying thud, then dried out iron-hard and further consolidated the porridged bricks in a most satisfactory way.

The clay that seemed to get everywhere was conveniently explained by the enthusiastic modelling classes and their proliferating statues of towering Loreleimädchen that stood about everywhere, ready to lure on sailors to their doom. Lorelei, as a Rhine nymph, had always been a girl of generous proportions in the poetic imagination of a better-nourished age and this quality was now accentuated to use up more clay and it was not scruples of modesty that now extended her hair to her knees. No one had ever remarked on the horrendous discrepancy between the amount of material supplied by the Red Cross and that consumed in statuary so that art continued undisturbed as the servant of life as the Führer had instructed. A sign-painter with a gift for Aryan folk art had painted pictures of yet more foaming, unlaced barmaids, 'Voll eingeschenkt!', at strategic points to distract the eyes of any randy Tommies passing near other things they should not see, such as the entrances to the tunnels.

But wood for shoring up the roof had been a major problem. The first solution had been to steal the oak benches stacked in the mess-hall and saw them up. All they needed to do was get the guards used to seeing them carrying the benches out into the yard to sit on them in the sun and carrying them back in the evening. It was easy to steal a few. They got the idea from a man who had lived in Tanganyika before the war where a similar technique was used for hunting monkeys attacking the crops of the fields. Three men would march in, observed by the sharp-eyed monkeys and only two would march back out, making a lot of noise but leaving one behind, concealed in the corn, to kill the monkeys when they resumed their ravages. Like Tommies, the monkeys were watchful but could not count. Then, it was as if there suddenly weren't enough places to sit down, though the number of prisoners remained the same. A new source clearly had to be found. Legs could be sawn off the bunk beds to lower them. So that the change would not be seen, they lowered every single one in the course of a day.

The greatest problem for an escape lay in the absence of geographical knowledge once the men were beyond the wire. Ingenious compasses had been prepared, using magnetised razor blades, fixed to pins and mounted so they could swivel on little blocks of wood. King C. Gillette would point the way. But the British had, as everyone knew, removed all the signposts from their roads which had done more to damage their war effort than anything the Germans could have done, so officers had swopped places with Other Ranks working around the camp to gain knowledge of the immediate area but that was as far as it went. Then a few had managed to get themselves assigned to longer expeditions. Security was so slack that often the work-party prisoners would be asked to keep guard to make sure no British officers turned up to surprise their escort who were off snatching a quick nap in the back of their truck. Several of the officers had managed to spend a splendid couple of days in a lumber camp, disguised as Other Ranks, with fine, hot food and fresh air, good as a holiday, going on long strolls to the tops of hills and keeping their eyes open on the trip there and back.

Still, he had hoped to be able to steal a proper map somewhere, through the activities of prisoners working around the camp offices but, thus far, nothing had materialised. As usual, he had urged everyone to greater efforts with bullyboy threats and promises. Then that young airman, Willy – the friend of that degenerate Todt man - had his moment of glory. He cheekily stepped forward at a meeting of the SS escape committee, saluted, and, grinning, ripped open his shirt to their astonishment, dropped his trousers and turned. There, on the shirttail, and carefully preserved since the day of their arrival, was a detailed map of the entire area, marking all rail links and major roads down as far as the south coast. The Great Western Railway had entirely forgotten to remove such maps that were displayed in every railway compartment alongside tempting, artists' impressions of romping, bucket-and-spade-wielding families at the seaside. The pictures had reminded Willy of the 'Strength through Joy' holidays to British resorts that Germans had confidently been encouraged to book, just a couple of years ago, in anticipation of victory. Most of the men had not even noticed the maps on the journey to the camp since the only thing prisoners ever look for on a map is home. He had simply traced one onto his shirttails with a fountain pen and now handed it over with ambassadorial aplomb and it would be swiftly copied by the Todt men through some cunning process involving the gelatine extracted from tinned jam. As he turned and bent to remove his dropped trousers and made to leave the room as a proud naturist, there was a roar of laughter. He had put on the shirt for the first time today, as Wenke suspected, simply for the theatre of taking it off before the rival SS and bending over and showing them his bare arse in alleged patriotic fervour. The map had transferred itself in negative to the skin of his behind, the entrance to the great Severn Tunnel being most appropriately placed. Even Wenke had managed a shark-toothed smile.

It had been decided that, when the time came, escapees would retain full military dress under civilianised greatcoats, thus affording them protection under the Geneva Convention that Wenke knew so well and had so often laboriously explained to the dull-witted camp commandant who steadfastly refused to display the regulations in every hut as laid down by law. The British would obviously be eager to gun them down in order take revenge for the killing by the SS of the British PoWs who had escaped from Stalag Luft III in March of that year and must be given no excuse, especially following the extensive use made of fake American uniforms in the glorious Ardennes offensive. This meant that none of the elaborate procedures of faking civilian clothing from military uniforms, used by the fleeing Tommies in the Fatherland, were necessary. As long as the weather remained cold, overcoats, with their shiny buttons removed, could hide just about anything.

♦ ♦ ♦

Private Morrison was not a happy man. Despite its promises of death or glory, the army had brought him little joy. Sergeant Wilson was on his case morning, noon and night – especially at night since that was when he was always on duty since their clash of wills. He was up before the commandant every week on some minor charge or other, on fatigues, extra duties, reduced pay. He began to dream of shooting Wilson. He imagined the raw terror in Wilson's nasty, little eyes, heard the promissory click of a cocked gun, the sweet detonation that would ease everyone's pain and the squeal as Wilson fell like a stuck pig. His mate, private Wills, was not faring much better, suffering from guilt by association. They weren't supposed to be here at a PoW camp at all, just waiting reallocation to a proper regiment. Every day he haunted the office, dropped the corporal a packet of fags, prayed and begged for the paperwork to come through.

'Any news, corp?'

A shake of the head. 'No son. Seems like there's some sort of cock-up back at Brigade.' He was, of course, under orders from Wilson to block any movement order.

The smug, little sergeant stepped through the door of the guardroom, so full of chubby self-satisfaction he could hardly breathe.

'Still here Morrison? Still here Wills? Well, you must like it here. Glad we are giving you such a nice time.' He tipped back his head to sneer and they saw the hairs quivering in his nostrils like little angry creatures. 'Let's see what we can do about that shall we? Time for a hut search, I think.'

No one ever searched the huts, not at six in the morning. In fact, apart from the random, personal inspections of the swill bins by the commandant at all hours of the day and night, British intrusions into German space were regular and predictable.

'Just us?' Wills protested. Morrison bit his lip. He wouldn't give him the satisfaction.

'Just you two lovely boys. Off you go. Now I'm going back for a nice little kip before my breakfast. Have a smashing time. I want a full search and detailed report on the orderly's desk by nine o' clock or I'll want to know the reason why. I know you like writing reports what with you being matriculated.' He smirked, lit a fag with deliberately slow gestures – Wait for it! Wait for it! and blew smoke in Morrison's face before swaggering off, stretching in theatrical anticipation of the delights of bed.

'But sarge...'

'Leave it, mate.'

They set off glumly across the still-dark parade ground, private Morrison boiling with rage and humiliation, knowing they would face nothing but further taunts and insults in the huts. The prisoners would be up and about their ablutions, taking every opportunity to bang into them and accidentally throw water and worse. They had been issued with rifles for guard duty and there was no one to sign them back in, so they kept them slung over their shoulders. Bugger regulations! As they approached the door of hut 16, there was already mocking whistling and clanging from lookouts.

'Fuck this!' snapped Morrison and unslung his rifle, booted the door open with a great cry and leaped through. Wills nervously followed, looking around. There was an immediate warm fug of male armpits, old farts, jammy feet, stale sperm. The prisoners were frozen in a tableau of surprise with the I-ain't-doin'-nothin'-Mum expression of guilty teenagers on their faces. The Tommies simply did not act this way. They had been carefully trained never to trespass unannounced. The only movement was from a man in underpants, nodding his head as he banged his tin mug on the table like a happy toddler at meal times. Morrison stepped forward, snatched it and flung it against the wall and threw the man back against the brickwork with the width of his rifle.

'Steady on, mate,' Wills whispered.

'On your feet, the lot of you.' He pointed his rifle at men sitting on bunks. They made eye-rolling, shrugging, we-do-not-speak, how-can-we-understand? gestures. He poked one in the stomach. '<u>Aufstehen</u>, Fritz.' Of course, he had been to the front, taken prisoners himself, learnt the necessary words and battle etiquette.

The spoken German magically made the man suddenly fluent in English. He stood up, clutching a towel slung around his waist. 'I am not Fritz. My name is Hans,' he said huffily and with affronted matronly dignity.

'All right then.' Morrison poked again and grinned horribly, 'If you prefer it. Hans up!'

They liked that. That was a good one. Ja, ja. They looked around at each other and smiled. This was the famous British humour? Hans up! Haha. Like Oscar Wilde, yes? The man raised his hands obligingly, grinning, and the towel dropped to the ground. Ooh la, la! More laughter at his girlish blushes. This was turning into a trouser-dropping French farce. You couldn't laugh with someone and stay furious, especially when they weren't really the ones driving you up the wall. It wasn't the friction of everyday life that made it possible to go on hating these people, it was the deliberate isolation that kept them from ordinary human contact. On the wall was a sad painting of a pouting, blonde girl in a blue dress, an object of pathetic male desire just like Morrison's own. It drew their eyes to it. God knew the last time he'd had any. He lowered the rifle and began to feel ashamed of himself, dropping his eyes to the floor. And then he saw something else.

There, in the corner, half-concealed by a bed, the otherwise-immaculate floor was covered with fresh dust like powdered concrete. He bent and looked closer, touched it, brought it up on his fingertips and smelt it. Around the edges of a sort of square, was yellow clay. He straightened, seized Hans's raised hand and lowered it to face level, as if about to deliver a gallant kiss or lead him delicately off onto the dance floor in his nice towel. Under the left arm was the tattoo signifying membership of the SS and there, beneath the nails, more sharp cement dust. He backed towards the door and raised the rifle. No smiles now. The eyes were hard. The hut had gone silent. Nobody moved.

'Go sound the alarm.' He spoke very quietly.

Wills was incredulous. 'The alarm? At this hour? Christ! What for? There'll be an awful stink. Wilson will have kittens.'

'Bugger Wilson. There's something not right here.' He waved the rifle back and forth, covering them all. 'They've been digging. Go sound the bloody alarm! Now!'

Wills scuttled off. After a while a distant wailing began and the whole camp erupted into teeming chaos like ants when their nest is disturbed by the nose of a probing aardvark. But in hut 16 still nobody moved.

◆ ◆ ◆

'It was entirely owing to the personal actions of Sergeant Williams that this dastardly plot was foiled. Acting within the framework of only the most general orders, this fine soldier instituted an unannounced dawn raid on his own initiative and implemented the search of the prisoners' quarters that resulted in the discovery of the tunnel, taking the enemy completely by surprise. Owing to his keenness and enterprise, his intuition and professionalism, a major escape was thus prevented that might have had serious consequences for national security. Sergeant Williams is an NCO with a sustained record of military achievement and serves as an example to the men under his command whose team spirit he has advanced immeasurably.

He is clearly first-class officer material and I have no hesitation in putting his name forward for a commission.'

Lieutenant Colonel Darling believed in giving credit where credit was due. He had arrived, fuming in a dressing gown, fully intending to give a dressing-down to whoever had created such a melodrama but was appalled to find clear signs of a tunnel, exposed and in a high state of completion. The greasy Security man had been right. When it was opened, they had discovered a distressed and naked prisoner trapped inside, nearly suffocated by the interruption of his air supply but fortunately there were present those with medical training who carried him out and refreshed his damaged lungs with a healing cigarette. There followed a full-scale search of the camp, all the prisoners paraded outside for roll call while the interiors were turned over with no respect given to rank or breakability of possessions. A number of clay sculptures were seized and smashed in the unfulfilled hope of finding hidden contraband. This was an operation that the troops greatly enjoyed as a settling of scores.

Since, in the First World War, Darling had been a PoW himself and successfully escaped from a German camp to rejoin his unit, he knew that tunnels were usually dug in pairs. The rather odd justification for this was that it allowed the second tunnellers to profit from the false sense of security created when the first were found. But the new search was effected as sloppily as the rest of the camp security. The second tunnel from hut 9 was not discovered though its design was identical to that of the first, nor were the false wall, the stores of civilianised overcoats, the forged documents, the maps and the ingenious compasses made of magnetised razor blades affixed to pins. The forbidden radios too were soon back in service, swamping the camp in rasping and fading Nazi propaganda that the Allies sought in vain to jam as the senders retreated ever-further south. And the only gap in the perimeter fence was found to have been made by the guards themselves so that they might more conveniently disappear unobserved to the village pub.

The next morning, Oberführer Wenke and friends marched into Darling's office but not to seek reconciliation or suffer rebuke.

'According to the terms of the Geneva Convention under which we are held, prisoners are permitted to attempt to escape so that any punishment whatever for such an endeavour is a violation of our military rights and you are cautioned that, in due course, it will be the subject of a formal complaint to visiting Red Cross representatives from the Protecting Power at the earliest opportunity together with the names of any officer responsible for such violation...'

'Get out,' said Darling wearily, letting his monocle drop from its socket. 'Get the hell out.'

♦ ♦ ♦

'How much longer do you think, Otto?' Slumped against the wall after being relieved at the mudface of Brünhilde, Willy was finally beginning to get excited. Behind his head was a sugary mural of a Horst-flavoured Bavarian landscape, a thing of sunlit mountains and lakes that evoked no homesickness in a North German city boy such as himself. For him, the tunnel was more of a therapeutic project than a political act. He had grown up knowing nothing but the Nazis and for him their regime was not something to fight for or a matter of choice, it was simply what there was - like the sun and the moon and stripes on pyjamas - and you made a life around its inevitability. But instead of just lying pointlessly entangled in barbed wire, watching his youth dripping away like water leaking from a rusty tank, he could invoke other measurements, see the tunnel growing, metre by metre, prop by prop, could see light at the end of it – a profitable investment of time, something that was literally going somewhere. With electric illumination and pumped ventilation, it was less scary down there than before, more like the sort of thing he had got up to with his brothers on their boyhood adventures romping in the heathlands around Hamburg. Two brothers. He felt his heartbeat surge. Both now dead and him living this crazy, stupid life with his grieving, widowed mother drinking coffee made from the acorns people used to feed to pigs. Somehow, with the thought of freedom, his claustrophobia in the hut grew worse, a clammy blanket pressed down relentlessly over his face. He rushed to the window and threw it open. His burnt hand was hurting again. A freezing wind was sweeping down through the camp, stripping the trees of any remaining leaves and leaving them shivering in nudity, jangling the barbed wire and rushing off blustering and unimpeded. Willy pressed his forehead to the icy glass and shakily breathed in its heavy, cold air.

Otto seemed not to notice. He shook his head. 'It all depends what we do at the other end. You can't have it coming up right by the wire. We have to go beyond the grass bank where there's a bit of cover but avoid tree roots that would make it too hard going. It's sloping up as we go so as to only leave a climb of a couple of metres at the exit point. It'll be tight.'

Horst closed his eyes and spoke dreamily. 'It would be great if we could wait till spring when there are leaves on the plants and some flowers about.'

Willy and Otto turned and looked at him, astonished.

'Not that I'm a Romantic poet,' he added hastily. 'I just mean it would offer more cover generally.' He paused and grinned. 'Still, a poem <u>would</u> be nice.' He began to quote a verse by Joseph von Eichendorff they had all learned at school,

'Wem Gott will rechte Gunst erweisen...' goose-stepping up and down and waving his arms about, gushing over the divine beauties of God's 19th century Nature and his own wanderlust in ranting Hitlerian cadences as if demanding territorial concessions from the deity. They all laughed.

Horst, Willy and Otto always worked their shift together. But how many of those beauties would be left by the time they got home? Despite the euphoric news that Wenke and the others were using to assault their ears, the BBC maintained a steady, understated tale of German retreat and calamity in a calm but ominous tone that had the ring of truth, with as many bombs and shells raining down on the Fatherland as Wenke claimed blessings from the Führer. In retaliation, one by one, the voices of the camp loudspeakers were stilled with thrown rocks and snapped cables. It was forbidden to read the British newssheets that were seized, ripped up and consigned to sanitary purposes, ending up stuffed down the throats of the lavatories before they could infect the camp with defeatism but it had been easy enough to reassemble the torn pages and Horst read them in the gloom of the latrines during artificially-long bowel movements. Wenke's answer to that had been to remove the cubicle doors and so the last shred of privacy from their lives. After all, there were precedents. Heretical thoughts were supposed to have first come to Martin Luther with the achievement of a prodigious bowel movement that succeeded a lengthy bout of constipation and had gone on to set fire to the world. The SS might be firm believers in the Thousand Year Reich but, for many of the others, it had always been a matter of what else could you do when your country was at war? The Allies were clearly advancing, which was a disaster, but what would the Russian barbarian hordes do to them if they ever reached Berlin? It was an unthinkable, unimaginable horror that must be stopped, compared to which everything else was a lesser evil. The whole camp was in a state of barely-suppressed, hysterical tension.

'And then what? After we get out. What happens then? Where do we go? What do we do?' It was not like Horst to be anything but as cheerful as a ricocheting sunbeam. 'I need to get home to look after my sister.'

The other two fell silent, a shadow fell across the room. Horst's sister lived in Dresden. There were terrible rumours about what had just happened in Dresden. The BBC crowed about it as a victory, the Germans as an atrocity that offset any possible small excesses of their own.

Willy turned from the window. 'Once we are free, then I am your secret weapon,' he said hoarsely but with pride. 'Your transport officer.' There had never been any question of their splitting up once through the wire, even though most had been formed into pairs and three men attracted attention in a way that two did not. Willy had spent sleepless nights thinking it through. 'The majority of the men will make straight for Swansea or other ports and try to steal boats or stow away to get to Ireland. Ireland is neutral but now interns combatants who end up on its shores, so they are merely swapping one camp for another, which is pointless. Most of them will be caught, especially if the alarm is sounded before they reach the port area and the British set up roadblocks. The cleverer ones will either hide nearby until the hue and cry dies down or jump a train and head in the opposite direction, towards the southern English ports, and try to get to a neutral country by masquerading as Dutch or Scandinavian sailors. We will do none of these things. We will go straight to an airfield and just take a plane. Our fighter ace, Hauptmann Franz von Werra, nearly got away with that a few years ago when he was captured. We shall succeed where he failed. He got the Iron Cross.'

'Nearly? How nearly?' Horst was a compulsive reader of small print.

Otto made a face. 'It was said at the time that a lot of that stuff he made up. Propaganda. Steal an aircraft? I think that's too difficult. A miss is as good as a mile. As for an Iron Cross...'

Willy flushed at this criticism of a fellow airman. Von Werra was one of his heroes and he treasured all knowledge about him. He had no earlobes and a pet lion named Simba. They had felt the same air under their wings. 'Why make an elephant out of a mosquito? He was sitting at the controls of a fighter with a British mechanic running him through the final startup procedure when they caught him. You can't get much closer than that. And you shouldn't jump to conclusions based on one event. You remember that when the <u>Titanic</u> sank, everyone switched from big liners to travelling in Zeppelins as they said they were safer. I think we would agree that they were wrong about that. Only heavier-than-air machines are the future.'

They frowned, their argument going down in flames. 'But could you fly one? A British plane?'

'Of course.' He smiled, happy on home ground, up in the air. 'All planes are much
the same. Aeroengines don't speak English or German, nationality is sausage to them. We are not trying anything very complicated. We wish to go up, navigate for a bit and come down again. I can do that with tomatoes on my eyes – though I promise I will keep them open for the peace of mind of you landrats.' His voice sank. 'Flying is not that hard. You know we used to go on missions sometimes quite drunk and there was never any problem as long as you dosed yourself up with Pervitin – amphetamine tank chocolate - to stop yourself falling asleep at the controls. The fact that there are three of us complicates things a little but can still be managed. Once we are airborne our chosen destination will depend on local circumstances.' He looked out of the window. There were cawing, black crows circling endlessly over the fresh-turned earth of the fields like the vultures over a corpse in North Africa– someone was ploughing out there - their destination depending on local circumstances. Like most young people, he equated freedom

with motion and to fly, liberated from the flat inevitability of the earth, was the most intoxicating form of liberty. Soon they would all three be free as birds.

Horst lay back and shut his eyes. 'Yes,' he murmured, seeing it all through closed lashes, 'I have never flown before.' He sat up, eyes shining. 'That's an exciting thought. It's like the invasion of Russia. What could possibly go wrong with such a simple plan?'

They all laughed. Then, in the distance, they heard a new sound, the sound of dogs barking.

◆ ◆ ◆

Lieutenant Colonel Darling's new and urgent requests for more resources, following the discovery of tunnel Bertha, had been simply ignored, thus bringing them into line with all his previous requests. The detection of the escape attempt, it was thought in Whitehall, firmly confirmed the adequacy of current security arrangements, and proved the wisdom of changing absolutely nothing. The whole thing was a matter for temperate self-congratulation rather than rigorous self-examination. A couple of failed subsequent attempts further reassured the authorities about the impossibility of the existence of another tunnel. Two PoWs had stolen the bars from a hut window and ingeniously sharpened them into a pair of crude wire-cutters. Once through the fence, they had made straight for the alluring Irish vessels of Port Talbot, hoping to contact along the way the forces of the Welsh resistance army that they were told flourished there. But when they arrived, they found the sea missing, lost amongst the sprawling industrial wasteland, so that they were arrested, undone by their failure to realise Port Talbot was not just the huge, bustling dock of their imagination, betrayed by treacherous English-language toponymy. Still, they had brought back useful local information and it would prove a sort of recce for the real breakout. Darling had reacted by instituting more thorough searches of the swill bins – to the disgust of the guards – haunted by the vision of escapees lurking beneath the murky surface and breathing through straws like the Red Indians in Boy's Own.

But the wheels within wheels of Whitehall's bureaucratic machine continued to spin randomly, pointlessly, grinding like the mills of God, till they snagged, engaged and finally coughed out a memo with even-handed disregard for reality and suddenly four huge guard dogs appeared, unannounced, at Island Farm, accompanied by two grim Scottish handlers in kilts and sporrans stuffed with raw meat rewards. They had long fangs, great hairy paws and their dogs took after them but there was no doubt that the prisoners were more afraid of these men in skirts than of the dogs. They were from Ross-shire but the prisoners had only picked up the word 'Russia' and knew them at once as the face of pitiless, Soviet vengeance, confirmed by their strange, unintelligible speech. Before the First World War, the animals themselves would have been called 'German Shepherds' but, caught in a battle between anti-German sentiment and the British love of dogs, had now emerged as 'Alsatians', further evidence of the contested identities tearing the Continent apart. Letters had appeared in the English papers, asking people not to be unkind to dachshunds. Otto took great pleasure in annoying the SS by pointing out their canine 'blood treason'.

Night and day, they ran busily up and down the wire, sniffing, pointing, growling, doing doggy things. To test them, a bold airman peed against the wire. When the dogs reached that part of their circuit, they went wild, barking, sniffing, turning around the spot and whining. Then they ran straight for the hut where the miscreant lived and attacked the door, snarling like the Hound of the Baskervilles, until their handlers called them off. The PoWs were impressed. Next, they tried making friends with the dogs to suborn their loyalties, offering them scavenged scraps of food but they would have none of it and fixed them with a cold, disdainful stare and lips curled back over their teeth – a little like the strange red-, yellow- and green-coloured local women who sometimes passed on the desolate road by the wire to be greeted with thunderous wolf-whistles, thrusting groins, acts of self-exposure and other male courtesies to which they remained strangely immune.

Those restlessly-questing canine noses were a source of anxiety to the diggers. Would they be able to smell out the tunnel? Fortunately, they were never taken inside the huts and surely the depth of the excavations would foil even their scenting powers. But they seemed obsessively interested in the area around which the planned exit would be dug, repeatedly tugging their keepers over to examine it, circling, tails erect. The prisoners thought of poisoning them but that would arouse suspicion and encourage reprisals, for the British were said to be sentimental about their dogs – as the Führer was about his own Blondi - and who knew what might come to replace them – searchlights? The solution appeared in the form of a large tin of curry powder, lid rusted with age, label peeling from damp, that they extracted from the neglected back shelves of the storehouse. Thrown through the wire and sprinkled around the exit area, it ensured that the dogs avoided it, skirted round it with their tails between their legs and resumed their patrol upwind of its fiery fragrance.

◆ ◆ ◆

Sundays were marked in the camp by religious services. Diversity of belief was not encouraged and the service on offer was like the food, a flavourless mix of anything that came to hand, stirred and boiled down. A small, ramshackle chapel had been built by the prisoners themselves out of scavenged materials and lavishly overdecorated in a lush Tyrolean pokerwork style that probably testified more to the PoWs' boredom than their piety. The cheapness of the materials encouraged rapid rot so that the little chapel soon exuded the musty smell familiar from centuries-old cathedrals and brought nostalgic tears to the eyes of the faithful. A lectern in the form of some kind of sculpted, clay water nymph had been suggested but refused.

Otto, having overcome Protestant scruples in the service of his art, had made an original donation of a painting of a suspiciously pin-up Madonna who looked as if she might have come to earth not from Heaven but the lurid fuselage of a crashed American bomber. The incumbent, Father Klotz, was necessarily multidenominational, a small, dark, Jesuitically furtive man whose ecclesiastical qualifications were allegedly no better than the identity documents being busily forged in the back rooms of the various huts. Many drew comfort from his services but the SS made no secret of their disapproval of such Jewish-tainted religion and there was constant bickering between the politicised 'German Christians', the traditional 'Confessing Church' and the Nazified 'Reich Church' that sought to replace the cross with the swastika and lay a gilt-edged, leather-bound copy of <u>Mein Kampf</u> reverently on every priestly altar. The Nazis had always recognised their kinship with an organisation that sought to control not just men's deeds but their most secret thoughts.

Otto's initial work of piety seemed to unlock something inside him and he now embarked on a whole series of pictures of the saints, an offering accepted by Father Klotz with alacrity as a believer in practical Christianity. In winter, the wind fair howled through the gaps in the walls of his little church as he huddled over a spirit stove and a few big plywood panels like these would really help keep it out. Otto found solace in the work, managing to somehow lock himself within the frame and so escape to another, distant world.

Saint Sebastian is often idealised in art as an icon of athletic male beauty, twisting in naked, agonised musculature - so much so that his admirers have often been suspected of unnatural tastes and faced many a cocked eyebrow. But in art, the mutilation of his divinely perfect body usually becomes a sort of blasphemy in itself, a further act against God and the glory of his entire creation. Otto would have none of this. He had always wondered why the human mind was so convincing when creating visions of Hell but could never come up with a decent Heaven that anyone would want to live in – National Socialists and Communists included. The achingly physical Saint Sebastian coaxed from his busy brush to be transfixed with arrows was hideously skinny in its skimpy breechclout and wearing rimless glasses over small, loveless eyes. The resemblance to Heinrich Himmler was unmistakeable. The conventional, corrugated abdominals of Sebastian were replaced by a starving man's importuning ribs and the empty folds of the loincloth suggested that the verse in that infamous English song about Himmler and the other Nazi leadership was nothing but the truth.

'You'll get yourself in trouble with the SS,' Horst and Willy had warned him, stepping back and appraising like appalled art critics. 'They don't like people to get too clever. Wenke went crazy over that clay model of Cologne cathedral, claiming it was giving information of use to enemy bomb aimers. They beat that bloke Stössel to death a couple of months back just for slipping an English nursery rhyme in his Christmas card:- "Adolf Hitler, Adolf Hitler, day by day your Reich gets littler." In the original, it was his balls got littler – you know how the English are obsessed with men's balls. Of course, he said it wasn't him, that some Tommy must have added it but they still beat the shit out of him and he died in the hospital the next day.'

'He died of heart failure.' Otto painted on.

'The guards logged it as "heart failure" to hush it up. Yeah, breaking every bone in his body made his heart fail sure enough. So please, please, watch yourself Uncle Otto.'

But Otto did not watch himself, smiled in enigmatic imitation of the Mona Lisa and busied away till lights out. It was as if a demon had gripped his brush and he had become the amanuensis of a higher power, a martyr not to the Christian faith but to art itself.

The next in the series was Saint Anthony of Padua, famed for his honeyed sermons, so that even fish gathered to listen to him when he preached beside the still waters and, when his coffin was opened hundreds of years after his death, his tongue was found to be beautifully preserved by the perfect and uncorrupted truth it had spoken. But his dress, according to Otto, was not the usual coarse monastic habit of the Renaissance masters that allowed an occasional glimpse of the hair shirt underneath, in which he spent years of wandering in poverty to carry the word to unbelievers. It was a garment both smooth and urbane and, instead of a monastic tonsure the hair was slicked and pomaded like praise poetry. The hawklike features were those of Josef Goebbels.

St. Valentine would have been surprised at the parallels between himself and Hermann Goering whose childhood was funded by gift-giving to his mother by a romantic Jewish patron whose adored mistress she became. Instead of having the usual body of a sere patriarch, the saint shown here was loathsomely corpulent, rolls of fat cascading down his belly and with greedy mouth and rapacious eyes looking out for its next meat meal. And how many would have known that the saint displayed at his throat, not the cross of crucifixion but the Iron Cross First Class?

The resemblance was obvious, only too obvious. Willy and Horst waited, headshaking, for the axe to fall.

It was only when Otto had launched himself on a fourth major work that the SS finally intervened. Saint Christopher was famed for his services in transporting thousands of those too weak to travel under their own steam. He had finally seen the true nature of his mission to God after originally dedicating himself to the more mundane service of the Devil. Needless to say, it came as a revelation to many that the saint was one of the few Christian martyrs to sport a toothbrush moustache and raise his arm in stiff but friendly blessing to the viewer.

They came at night, the stuff of nightmares, as they always did, Wenke and three rat-faced henchmen, hardly visible in their lush black. They came without clubs, showing that this was a mere preliminary visit but still cast a pall of fear and silence about them. Otto was working, crouched on the stark concrete, touching in highlights to Saint Christopher's left boot under the bare bulb while Willy and Horst watched in hushed fretfulness. Wenke surveyed the painting leant against the wall, hands on hips, sucked on his lower lip and began fisting his own left hand. The Führer had been a keen art critic and this was the moment for some active art education.

'So it's true. There's been talk,' he said ominously.

'In a prison camp, there is always talk, Herr Oberführer. What kind of talk is that?' Otto's spoke smoothly, eyes gleaming with choirboy innocence. Wenke had always been down on him – from the time he pointed out that sailors and airmen don't decide to surrender, that choice being made for them once their ship or aircraft goes down under them. Only land soldiers like Wenke had the luxury of actively choosing to give in. Only land soldiers could therefore be judged and reproached. And only airmen and sailors were likely to have information useful to the enemy and so subject to unpleasant interrogation. Captured SS were regarded by the Allies as useless and Otto had made it unspokenly clear he shared that view.

'Listen you, cut the crap.' There was something about Otto that reminded him of the degenerate and scruffily defiant Edelweisspirates, those spoiled libertines who had opposed the Führer in the early days. Well, they had been brought to jackbooted heel most satisfactorily. 'According to the terms of... that is to say, I would remind you that any offences committed in this camp will be subject to comradely admonitions and will be noted and form the basis of prosecution and punishment in the Fatherland after the war where the families of traitors may also be held jointly responsible. Is that supposed to be the Führer or not?'

All three knew what 'comradely admonitions' were - a euphemism for being fearfully beaten within an inch of your life, indeed within a millimetre, in a hail of sticks, ropes and fists. They were more popularly known as 'holyghostings' and carried out in anonymous darkness, with the victim being asleep at the start as the guardians of authority pounced on him, and either unconscious or dead at the end.

'As usual, Oberführer, you go right to the heart of the matter. I congratulate you on your keen eye.' Otto paused and his brush became a conductor's baton, pointing out features. 'You will note that, in accordance with the Party's views, the style is clearly Aryan with no hint of offensive degeneracy – no impressionism, expressionism, fauvism, surrealism, Dadaism - though I am grateful to all such schools for establishing that talent is not necessary to be a successful artist. What do you think?'

'The Führer, yes or no?' Wenke rasped and took a step closer.

Otto smiled. 'That is a question that defies simple binarism. You see, there is a point at which every really interesting question tips over into philosophy. That is the point at which it dissolves itself and disappears. First, let me ask you. Is it not the case that the enemy forbid the use of any of the proud symbols of our Party and nation within the camp? No swastikas, no portraits that honour our beloved leaders?'

'That is the case. But I do not see...'

'Imagine, then, that a man's patriotic fervour was so great that he yearned to openly display them, and in a context appropriate to blissful contemplation. Might he not choose to do so inside a place of dignified worship, replacing the old symbols of hope with the new and thus sneaking them in under the very noses of the foolish foe through useful ambiguity?'

Wenke pouted and puffed out his chest. 'We in the National Socialist Party reject the Christian Church as a false, non-Aryan faith. Portraits of our leaders have no place there.' The others nodded vigorous agreement and gave what sounded like an imitation of the guard dogs' growl.

Otto furrowed his brow in mock puzzlement. 'Indeed? Then does that mean you are in disagreement with the Führer? You mean that all Catholics should immediately take down his picture from their walls? Surely not! Are you opposed to the Reich Church that he himself established? That cannot be! Are you saying that that great masterpiece, <u>Mein Kampf</u>, should <u>not</u> be displayed on its altars in counterpoint to the Bible as a statement of faith?' He put his hand to his mouth. 'Oh no! Have we simple souls offended? Should we not have sent our beloved leader a Christmas card with its implied Christian message? I understood that was approved personally by yourself.'

They shuffled and mumbled. 'No, no. This is playing with words.'

Otto shook his head and began picking out contrasts in the saint's holy moustache with a fine brush. 'Are you claiming that the Führer was not sincere when he signed his Concordat with the Pope and agreed to religious toleration? I have always believed that the Führer cannot lie.'

Wenke was not used to arguing with words so much as with fists. 'Look, you worm, the other paintings we let go. If you continue with this one, I'll nail you to the wall.'

Otto looked bewildered. 'What then would you have me do with it, Oberführer?'

'Destroy it. Burn it.'

Otto gaped in comic disbelief but the tears in his eyes seemed real enough. 'You are ordering me to insult the Führer by destroying his image? Burn it? Like a Jewish-Bolshevik book? I can't believe my ears. I simply cannot do such a thing.'

Wenke stepped forward and raised his fist to strike the panel, then wavered as the Führer's eyes rested on him accusingly. He was too high up to switch the punch to Otto, so he stepped back and gave him a great kick instead. He would have loved to do more, come down on him like a Panzerfaust, but they needed his engineering skills for the tunnel.

'You piece of shit! I've got my eye on you. Just watch it.'

The other three sneered and it seemed they were about to add their own kicks, then thought better of it as they would then have to run to catch up with Wenke who was already clip-clopping arrogantly towards the door.

'Yeah! Just watch it!'

As they left, Horst shook his head. 'How is it possible for a man to be angry all the time and 'have hair on his teeth'? The trouble with Oberführer Wenke is he is as mad as a bagful of badgers, sometimes gets above himself and thinks he is the real Führer.'

'Actually, 'Otto grinned. 'It's the other way round. Our great leader sometimes shouts and screams because thinks he's Oberführer Wenke. And anyway,' he laid the brush down across his knees and smiled, 'let me ask you a question I have been pondering. What is the difference between Christ and the Führer?' It was said in the tone of voice that marked it as a joke.

They looked blank.

'With Christ, it was he that died for all of us.'

The next day, Saint Christopher joined the other saints in the brave, little church but at the end of the week Father Klotz, after a visit from Wenke, decided abruptly that it was his dearest wish that the chapel should become a gymnasium for the exclusive use of the SS and that he would henceforth make do with the mess-hall for his services and distribute the host in the smell of cold stew. People could not help noticing that he had a black eye and a limp, something that Wenke and the other SS seemed to find extraordinarily funny as they ate watchfully at their separate high table.

The friends considered these Christian stigmata in whispered undertones. 'I think,' said Horst, 'that we should finish off that tunnel as soon as possible, Uncle

Otto, and get you through it before Wenke and his friends run out of other people to beat up.'

Otto nodded. 'You may be right. What you are saying is that I should flee Britain and claw my way back to Germany not to get away from the Tommies but to escape from crazy Nazis. That sounds like eminent good sense to me.'

♦ ♦ ♦

'We're through!' It had fallen to Horst's team to make the final breakthrough and open Brünhilde to the world. Tunnelling vertically up to the surface had been the hardest part. Horst felt the sailor's familiar terror of drowning. Every shovelful fell in your face and, at any point, the whole lot could come down on your head as the putty of soft clay turned back to loose, black soil. The lights had been turned off so as not to give the game away and he pounded blindly at the earth above him like a man accidentally buried alive and trying to tear his way out of the grave, his own fear screaming in his ears like when he was shut in the torpedo tube. It seemed as if it would go on forever and then there was a cascade of something wet in his face and stars appeared blissfully overhead. They were the same stars you saw from inside the wire but, being outside the wire, they were transformed. The air was wonderfully fresh after the suffocating tunnel and he gulped it down till he felt his racing heart slow and the sweat begin to cool on his skin. A wind stirred and the chill in the air gave it a hint of the English seaside. Above all, it smelled of freedom which was surprisingly the same as the smell of ripe farmyard manure from the pens next door. Here, there was no familiar periscope, so Horst poked his head up carefully and looked around. They were right on target, beyond the grass bank and at the edge of a field, with enough hedge cover to make them almost invisible from the camp if they kept low. Now the exit had to be concealed well enough not to be spotted all next day. It could be enlarged when they made their final break. Again, luck was on their side. There was a big, flat stone right by where they had come up, gleaming in the moonlight. He wrestled it across and let it drop over the mouth of the hole. It hit him on the head.

'Ouch! <u>Scheisse</u>!'

He tumbled back into the tunnel and lay there, just wheezing with choked laughter, waiting for the bone ache to ebb from his back. Anxious whispers echoed along the

shaft like scuttling spiders.
'It's fine,' he called back hoarsely. 'Bullseye! Hole in one!'

♦ ♦ ♦

CHAPTER FIVE

Preparations had been slowly winding up for days. More attentive guards might have noticed the curious phenomenon of the prisoners talking to each other using rather more English than was usual. Most of the officers had at least a smattering from school and classes had been organised for Other Ranks, not in the hope that they could pass for natives, but as friendly Dutch or occupied Scandinavians whose languages, it might safely be assumed, no casual passer-by would speak. They bristled with suitably meaningless documents and passes. A considerable windfall had come in the form of an overcoat purloined from the Great Western Railway. Its embossed brass buttons with all their heraldic floskelry, rolled in ink, provided a plausible, official-looking stamp for Norwegian identity papers.

'I am a sailor from Oslo and seeking the harbour. Please to tell me the way back to my sheep.'

'I thank heartily. This food smacks very good. I am so hungry to the point that I could eat a horse.'

'Are you safe that this is the train after Swansea?'

And secretly, over and over. 'I am a German officer prisoner of war and I capitulate myself to you. I am a German officer prisoner of war and...'

◆ ◆ ◆

Farmer Davies had never enjoyed the spotlight of fame. His had been a slow and rural life in tune with the seasons of the year where most of the people he had truck with were relatives and Swansea was the furthest extent of exotic travel. He was puzzled and a little self-conscious to be the principal object of interest to so many of the PoWs as he drove his tractor up and down the field on a bright spring day, getting the rough work done and practising for the annual ploughing competition next week. He was a champion ploughman and lived in terror of being bested at farm work by one of those silly Land Army girls or brawny lumberjills who seemed to be everywhere these days. He watched the Jerries watching him, fascinated, through the wire and felt his cheeks glow red with coy embarrassment. He did not like the inmates, no one did. The only advantage they brought was the swill for the pigs and the quality of that had rather gone down lately. Unlike the Italian lads, the Germans were aggressive and arrogant and he hadn't had a decent night's sleep since they moved in, what with all the singing and shouting and banging. And all that was bad for the sheep too. The rate of miscarriages had rocketed since they arrived. Sometimes they jeered at you from inside the camp and made gestures that were doubtless rude if you were a Jerry and knew what they meant but they were silent today. On a reflex, he checked his flies were done up. He hadn't shaved this morning and was conscious of the grey stubble on his chin. Perhaps it was the tractor that attracted them. It was far from new but he'd heard they still used horses for ploughing in Nazi Germany so maybe they'd never seen this sort of modern thing before. Or maybe they were just pathetic townies who knew no better. He gave them a neighbourly wave and a smile as he was at the closest point at the end of the field but they just stared back sullenly with their hands thrust in their trousers, playing pocket billiards like as not, which annoyed him. He executed a particularly fine swerve round a large, flat stone over by the bank and he could see that that impressed them and he laughed at the expectant looks on their silly faces. They'd thought he would hit it and smash his chisel or mainshare. Well sod them if they couldn't be a bit more friendly. To be friendly cost nothing, after all. The only good thing about them Nazzies was those long, leather overcoats you saw them stamping about in on all the newsreels. He'd fancy one of them for the wind and the rain. He set off grumpily towards the bottom of the field, shaking his head, and the crowd melted away. Such was the brevity of fame.

♦ ♦ ♦

Lieutenant Colonel Darling thought he looked rather fine in his dinner jacket and stole a sly admiring glance at himself in the etched mirror over the fireplace. The jacket had shrunk a little during the war years and tightened around the waist, which was surprising given the shortage of rations, but stodgy army food would do that to you. At least, careful wardrobing and the attentions of his batman had assured it had been spared by moths which was more than could be said for the clothes of some of the other gentlemen on show tonight. More than one sported a buttonhole badge to mask the moth holes on silk lapels. He had toyed with coming in full military dress uniform but that would have made him distastefully prominent and he was a man who wore clothes to blend in, not to stand out.

They did you a decent enough dinner at the Conservative Club, the cook was as clever at disguising cheap scraps as fine cuisine as any Froggie chef and, with the members' diverse connections, laying hands on plenty of booze was never a problem. But it all proved the sad truth that everything these days was a shabby imitation of something else, that wartime life was a cheap cardboard parody of real life. His eyes came to rest on the legs of a woman across the room, not out of any sexual attraction – she was the recipient of the attentions of a retired admiral who had remarked, 'I can't stand to see a woman left unmanned in the course of a war'. It was simply that she had drawn wobbly black lines up the backs of them in imitation of the seams of the silk stocking she could no longer afford. It was a pathetic pretence that fooled no one and reflected an entire world as false as Charlie Chaplin's moustache. Everyone was 'marking time', which was an odd expression because it meant time was unremarkable. He felt deeply depressed.

This was not the most political of Conservative Association branches, mostly just a place where the people who really ran things could get to know each other – the bank manager, the magistrate, the besuited and dentured classes of the town. Darling had never been any good at using the informal levers of power. Since the beginning of the war, he had felt himself accumulating a certain unwilled rigidity that had invaded his spine, making him cold and inflexible and he was aware of human traffic moving around him like a roundabout. He had no social conversation. Language, for him, was a tool for conveying information or expressing irritation. Perhaps his response was just part of the war where all news seemed to be bad news and you stiffened yourself in readiness for the next blow. Perhaps that would change now that it was clear, after all the false dawns, that the war really was coming to an end in what the Americans called slow 'meat-grinder' advances across both Germany and Asia and with Hitler shooting more German generals than the Allies could. But then, the coalition would be over and party politics would be back with a vengeance, as the different groups tore at each other's throats. The smile on Winston Churchill's photograph over the door was already looking more like a snarl every time he looked at it.

There was a tap on his shoulder. 'Edwin. I've been meaning to have a word with you.' A measured, plinketty-plonk, Welsh voice used to delivering bad news.

He looked round. His face fell further. Police Superintendent May and in swanky full-dress uniform. 'Hello, Brother William.' They swapped a joke Masonic handshake. He sighed. 'I imagine it's about escapes from the camp again. As I think I said, we have that matter well in hand.' That came out with more truculence than he had intended but he had actually been holding May's empty hand at the time so...

May made a face. He had a face fit for the making of faces, long and hardened by weather and other people's bad experiences and listening sceptically to recitations of poor evidence by junior officers. He sloshed the contents of his glass – doubtless unalcoholic - in a this-way, that-way gesture of unconviction. 'The last escape was not detected for twenty-four hours, Edwin. As I have explained, that makes the odds of a swift recapture very much less and the difficulties expand exponentially with time elapsed. If those men had got on a ship...'

Darling screwed in his monocle and glared. He didn't like being told how to do his job by a scrimshanking civilian who couldn't find a shag in a fag factory and gunned him down with a few hard declarations. 'We have new arrangements since the discovery of the last escape attempt. We have a midnight as well as a morning roll call. The dog patrols alone make it very unlikely any runners would get so far nowadays. We'd have 'em back in their cages in the twinkling of an eye.' He twinkled a steely, monocled eye in proof. 'Our procedures have been tightened across the board. It's impossible for any camp to be totally secure but I think the shooting of those escapees from that PoW camp in Staffordshire the other day will have cooled down the hotheads and shown them we mean business. You can be sure I made certain the inmates heard all about that. Moreover, there has been a change of mood in the camp, a new spirit of co-operation. The tunnel was a remnant of the way things were. With our armies pressing forward and defeat imminent, why would anyone think it even worth the effort to escape?' A note of rare enthusiasm crept into his voice. 'There is what you might call a cultural Renaissance in the camp, paintings blossoming on the walls everywhere, great clay sculptures. They do these mermaid things. So realistic! - if a mermaid can be realistic. You know, they even seem to smell of the river. I am thinking of organising a little exhibition and I hope you will come. As for escape, well, you don't paint the house in the morning if you are planning to jump off the roof in the afternoon.'

May nodded. 'That's fine, Edwin, as far as it goes but we need more detailed planning. I've had my people work out a step-by-step schedule of procedures that can be implemented immediately in the case of an emergency, including the siting of key roadblocks and an escalating series of responses according to the time lost since the escape. I think it's important this should remain entirely a police matter to avoid the panic that might be caused by the sudden appearance of armed troops on the streets. It is crucial that we should receive prompt information of any attempt since the success of my plan depends on throwing a tight cordon around the camp at a distance of three miles to maximise concentration of forces. According to my calculations...'

Darling yawned and tuned out. He knew May was a great one for his bloody plans. He had been to his office once and seen his plans for floods, parachutists, gas attacks, civil insurrection, explosions at the bomb factory, an invasion by the Irish and probably for earthquakes, tropical typhoons and The Second Coming too, if the truth were known. He nodded, nodded and sneaked a look at his watch. One more snort and he would head for home and bed. He hoped there wouldn't be more bloody choral singing tonight. The Krauts were worse than the Welsh for that.

♦ ♦ ♦

It was a fine but moonless night and a sudden chill had set in that promised an ironhard frost in the morning. Farmer Davies had read the signs of the coming weather in the wizened hank of old seaweed like a witch's hair that he kept hanging on the barn door and to which he attributed almost magical powers of prediction, so that by dark the sheep were all safely gathered in.

The evening began with a concert in the improvised camp theatre with lots of loud singing, hand-clapping and foot-stamping to camouflage the noise as the unguarded food store was broken into and rifled with the tinned rations seized and distributed. There had been a broad, Berliner comedian with lots of arse jokes in gross dialect, a willowy Marlene Dietrich/ Lily Marlene impersonator, clinging to a cardboard lamppost, whose batting eyelashes had provoked lust and patriotic rage in equal measure and a fine tenor who had led them in the stonking Horst Wessel to bring the curtain down. The Tommies had been primed to listen for Silent Night but Christmas was well over. The escapers had to wait until after the new midnight roll call that had been instituted following the discovery of hut 16's tunnel but the guards were amazed at how quickly that had gone, with every possible co-operation from the PoWs and none of their usual tiresome shenanigans. They must be in a good mood after the concert. It was a good sign it would be a quiet night, a rare chance for the sentries to charm one of them sugary Nazi stroodlebuns out of the fat cooks over at the Germans' bakery and get their feet up with a cuppa before dawn.

♦ ♦ ♦

The men moved noiselessly across the compound in groups of five, dark ghosts, taking cover in the pools of black shadow behind the huts. Since the guards at the perimeter always stood at exactly the same points to shelter from the prevailing cold wind, it was easy to avoid them and their sightlines. The escapers had been rigorously checked – clothes, documents, suitcases- for giveaway signs and issued with Willy's Great Western Railway maps and waited in order of assessed viability as escapees. The recent attack on Dresden had led the Irish – ever eager to stir the English pot - to offer a more general asylum to escaping Germans. Many of the men had rerouted their travel plans accordingly and felt a renewed urgency to get home by heading across the Irish Sea, which was entirely in the opposite direction to home, but perhaps Irish ships might now be more openly sympathetic to not noticing 'stowaways'. The latest unofficial news was that rampaging Allied armies had crossed the Rhine and were driving much deeper and faster into the heart of Germany than even pessimists had expected. God knew what contesting armies might be doing to the civilian population, like heedless drunks swaying and punching, brawling in a bar fight and smashing everything around them.

Final preparations had been made. The tunnel was scrupulously lined with rags so that the escapees' clothes would not be marked out by stains of mud and clay. The earth around the exit spot had been freshly spiced and marinated with curry powder for the benefit of the dogs. Faces were blacked up with soot as in a commando raid, bringing back memories of days of active service - the querulous stomach in the nervous wait for zero hour before the first rifle shot of a pre-dawn attack, a final, shaking cigarette that you knew might well be your last on earth in a silence that was deafening. Yet the men looked at each other with eyes that shone happily with a tension and excitement they had not known all year in a war that had ceased to have any greater goal and become merely a matter of dull habit. They felt really alive, drunk with energy for, apart from anything else, this was one hell of a lark. It was important to get going as early as possible, giving the longest possible gap before the alarm was raised. But then there was a collapse at the tunnel mouth, hasty reinforcement of the opening, desperate clearing of landslips and it was fully 3pm before the lights flashed their 'Go' signal and the first group dropped, like leaping paratroopers from a plane, down into the hole. Lookouts, posted all over the camp, kept a sharp watch for approaching sentries and the lights functioned as a warning system. When they went out, everyone froze. When they flashed back on, the steady flow through the tunnel resumed.

They could not believe how easy it was. Group after group jumped into darkness and simply disappeared as if in a magic trick. A blackout curtain had been hung over the exit shaft and the chief concern was that the frost forming on the grass might crisp it up and make it rustle and crackle underfoot as the men moved swiftly away from the fence. Yet, the hours passed and still they streamed down the hole and out into the world in a steady trickle. How long should they continue? It seemed to Wenke as he stood, waving his arms over the entrance like a crazed conductor, that they could empty the whole camp if they wanted to but that was pointless since most of the inmates were unprepared and had no documents or food and now the prime concern had to be to try to put off the moment of discovery as long as possible. When should they call a halt? Wenke peered through a gap in the shutters. It was still usefully dark outside. With his back turned, the matter was resolved by a single unauthorised opportunist, Leutnant Heinz Tonnsmann, who seized his chance and his brilliant white kitbag and simply dived for the opening. Things had reached that point in the abandoning of a ship where those in charge of the process have themselves gone overboard, every man for himself now, with all pretence of order lost. Struggling through the tunnel, its rag lining well churned up with the boots of the dear departed, Tonnsmann popped out of the hole with a grunt and was halfway to the cover of the trees, clutching his big, bright, shiny bag, when a shout went up. There came a Crack! and he found himself flat on his back with an agonising pain in his shoulder and then, a minute later, the hot muzzle, not of a gun, but of a great slavering dog in his ear. He raised his hands, pointlessly, as he was lying on the ground and then came screams, more shots and hysterical laughter. He looked up, expecting to see a scene of carnage, blood, thrusting bayonets and chortling English guards. But no. Two pursuing Tommies had fallen down the hole and nearly shot each other as their rifles went off. The prisoners hiding in the bushes had given themselves away with their hysterical laughter at the classic Chaplinesque pratfall and were soon being rounded up, still laughing helplessly, beneath humourless rifle butts. Nobody seemed to bother about Tonnsmann, as he was clearly going nowhere and it was some ten minutes before the camp commandant came stomping towards them along the wire, screaming, in a greatcoat over his striped pyjamas, for all the world stumbling like a drunk, while Wenke stood at the open shutters of hut 9, safely behind the fence in full uniform, shouting, 'According to the terms of the Geneva Convention, under which we are held....'

It was clear to Tonnsmann, as he lay bleeding and neglected in the icy mud, that Wenke had never been so close to being simply shot. The cold air zithered with lethal possibilities. The dog lifted its head and watched the chaotic scene over its shoulder with frank curiosity at all these snarling humans and then turned back and, almost as a shrugged afterthought, bit Tonnsmann in the ear, quite badly.

◆ ◆ ◆

The telephone rang and Corporal Crookshank appeared at the door, tousled and unshaven. He was beyond the age where such an appearance looks endearing. 'A Superintendent May for you, sir. On the blower. Says it's urgent.'

Darling groaned. 'Tell him to go and f...No. Best put him through. Tea!' He picked up the receiver and there followed a series of clicks and buzzes and the small, hectoring voice was needling in his ear.

'What the hell's going on, Edwin? We can hear the racket from here – alarms, shots, screaming and shouting.' The voice was hesitating between concern and outrage.

'There is no cause for alarm.'

'It's my job to say that and when I do there is usually every cause for alarm if not outright panic. What the hell is going on up there?'

'There was an escape attempt tonight.'

'Attempt you say. So no one's actually missing? It was a failed attempt, then?'

He grunted, 'A small number of men got under the fence through a tunnel. They were immediately detected and rounded up within yards of the wire and are all safely back under lock and key. One man was wounded and is receiving care in the camp hospital but nothing life-threatening. You may take it that the affair is effectively over.' He made to hang up but May's voice came back tinnily.

'Nevertheless, it would have been helpful to have been kept in the picture. I should have thought that after our conversation of this evening...'

'Yes, yes.' Testily, 'There was no point in telling anyone anything until we had established exactly what had happened.'

'What's that noise I can hear?'

'It's nothing. Rather, it's the prisoners acting up, banging, stamping, shouting. They do it to annoy and create confusion whenever something they don't like happens. You get used to it. We just ignore it though the neighbours complain endlessly. There's nothing we can do. Under the terms of the Geneva Convention, under which they are held...' Of God, Wenke had got inside his head.

'I've put all my Specials and Auxiliaries on standby. I think I'd better come out there.'

Darling was stiffly unwelcoming. 'As you wish. We are naturally keen to show every courtesy to the civil authorities but I assure you there is absolutely no need. The matter is well in hand. The prisoners are all accounted for. We have held a roll call and everyone has answered to their name.'

There was a stunned silence. 'Answered to their name, is it?' You could almost hear him shaking his head in disbelief over the wire. God almighty! Hadn't Darling been to a school where they took register and the boys knew how to have their fun with a dozy master by answering for each other? 'I'll come out straight away.'

May put down the telephone and, as he did so, it rang again while still in his hand. It was a call from Llanharan police station. 'Got a couple of your Nazee lads here, sir, from Bridgend. A bit cold and sleepy and sorry for themselves they are. They say they are officers and want to catapult themselves to us, whatever that means. If they've been mislaid, would you like them back?' The tone of scorn was unmistakeable. May sat bolt upright.

'Tell me.'

The local police had picked up two escaped SS officers, wandering through the darkened streets in the early hours after being shunted about pointlessly in goods trains, some crammed full of wobbling explosive shells and having decided that the risk to their lives from such unreliable ordnance was just too great. The escapees, big men and trained to kill with their bare hands, had immediately surrendered when challenged by a lone, young constable on night patrol – he coming upon them unobserved as his bicycle lamp was not working. Assuming he was armed to the teeth as he would have been in Germany, they meekly accompanied him and his bicycle to the station where they were given a cup of tea generously made with the condensed milk you could only get on special ration and normally kept for visiting VIPs. Being used to German forms of policing, it was impossible for them to believe that British bobbies were sent out alone, equipped with no more than a stick and a flickering torch and that that menacing bulge under the constable's rain cape was not a cocked tommygun. When the escapees were searched, their pockets and haversacks were found to be weighed down with stocks of tinned army bully beef and cigarettes, real coffee and cocoa, like black market traders – all exotic, mouthwatering stuff their civilian captors hadn't seen in years. Naturally, in a farming area, there was always a certain amount of leakage into the informal trading sector that prevented shopkeepers exercising the same brutish tyranny that they enjoyed in the cities but sophisticated factory produce was worth its weight in gold and unobtainable. Each also had tucked away for emergencies a puzzling pair of comfy bedroom slippers – that would be sliced up to attempt to find their true and hidden meaning - but had not thought to bring the vital keys to the corned beef or any other form of tin-opener.

'Well now, I think we'd better hang on to all those supplies – vital evidence you see. But you can have the men back directly like if you're so minded.'

The word of their booty spread rapidly through the force and SS prisoners would become literally prize captives for their police hunters who salivated like hungry cannibals at the mere sight of them, thinking of the treats they might be carrying.

♦ ♦ ♦

'It works with sheep, Edwin, and I find that what works with sheep usually works with prisoners by hook or by crook.'

Superintendent May was a local man of rugged, hill-farming stock. They had marched every single PoW through a small gate, one by one, and counted them properly, checking them off by name against the record cards and putting a dab of red dye on their hand like ewes that had been freshly tupped, just to make sure they knew who had and who hadn't been counted. The prisoners were deliberately milling around, trying to confuse matters, shouting for their breakfasts and making loud, bleating noises, both irritating and distracting, to show that they had seen the similarity too and rejected it. Attempts were made to steal some of the cards by mobbing the table. No point. Sergeant Wilson slashed at their fingers and the red dye did not lie. Darling had watched the stack of cards shrink down steadily through the early morning but there was still a good, thick pile left over - even after they had removed the eleven recaptured, laughing their heads off, in Farmer Davies's freshly-ploughed field. Superintendent May thought Edwin Darling looked proper sheepish, himself.

'So what's the bad news?' Darling looked out over the sea of still-smirking PoWs, monocle dangling in limp despair, as Corporal Crookshank totted up and shoved his pencil crisply behind one ear.

'Looks like 70 is still missing, sir.' Said with a certain joyful malice - Crookshank, remembering all the times the CO had troubled his peace, couldn't resist using the military word that was like a knife in the back. 'Bit of a shambles really, sir.'

Darling groaned. 'Jesus Christ!'

May – being chapel - frowned at the blasphemy but lay a consoling hand on his arm. 'No! Only 68, old man, counting the two caught in Llanharan. You see? Look on the bright side. Even in the darkest hour, there is always a gleam of light and things are never as bad as they seem.'

Darling had the impression the policeman was about to break out in a hymn and fatigue overwhelmed him with the sin of despair. 'Hell's bells! Sometimes I wonder what the point of it all is. What's it all for?'

May brightened. 'Now there I can help you, Edwin. I saw a really helpful film entitled precisely that, just the other day. Something by the Crown Film Unit, it was. Very informative, I thought. You should watch that.'

♦ ♦ ♦

CHAPTER SIX

Superintendent May had a plan for all this, prepared well in advance. He had plans for everything and lists, and random information of all sorts tucked away for emergencies. A thick cardboard file contained reports on the articulation of washing lines throughout the area. It had been pointed out that local ladies arranged their washing lines with geographical regularity so as to catch as much sunshine as possible, which might allow them to unwittingly serve as a sort of improvised compass for invading German forces. He had been about to launch an ambitious programme of rerandomization of lines when some snotty, lickspittle - a greasy, little man from Security who refused to identify himself as he was from Security - had come down from Whitehall and quashed it like a bug by maintaining that the same information could be gleaned by just looking up at the sun. His own objection that this was Glamorgan and sunshine was a rare commodity, was summarily dismissed with bland arrogance. Never mind. He had hung on to the plan just in case.

What he needed now was the camp escape plan – dramatically named Plan X. Only he could activate it, of course, since he had written it in code and stamped it Top Secret and no one else could make head or tail of it. He rubbed his hands together in glee, teased it out from among the whole drawerful of other plans in his filing cabinet, spread it over his desk and looked it over afresh, remembering all the hours of work that had gone into it. Naturally, it was quite useless now. The whole thing had been predicated on the alarm being sounded immediately following an escape and, instead of that, Darling had given the runaways a free pass for the entire night. They could be spread out all over the county and beyond, be well on their way to London or Dublin by now, be bathing off the beaches of south Glamorgan or having a fine breakfast in a posh Bristol hotel. What could have been so simple would now have to be a major manhunt. Wonderful! There would have to be roadblocks, searches of all trains – passenger and goods - passing through the area, extra security at sites of possible sabotage and the major rail terminals in all cities, scouring of woodlands, outbuildings, dramatic warnings to the public to immobilise vehicles and bring bicycles indoors at night. Endless disruption and interference! The original idea had been to keep the public out of it. Now, he had no choice. They would have to be the very eyes and ears of his whole operation. He reached for the telephone and called the BBC in Cardiff. After talking to several, irritating women who refused to believe who he was, he got through to a chum in the news room and briefed them in clear, concise terms on what had happened and what the public response should be.

He hung up and stepped back to admire his handiwork. Everyday life would now have to be put on hold while he organised, directed and collated everything like the general he knew, deep down, he was destined to be. It was a pity the Home Guard had been recently disbanded or he would have called them out immediately. He could still have a go. Many had not yet handed in their kit and he would see if the remnants could be flushed out. This was not a time for penny-pinching. There was a well-placed fellow mason who could be called into service. First things first.

'WPC Shawcross!'

A stout, blonde woman appeared in the doorway hobbling on sensible shoes, flushed and smoothing her skirt over thick legs. 'Yes sir?'

'Take the petty cash and go down to Woolworths. Buy a large tin of dressmaker's pins. Buy two if necessary. Don't forget to get a receipt even if they have to summon the manager. Draw up a grid of seventy 1inch squares of paper, inside each draw a swastika on both sides and glue each square to a pin.'

'Uh?' She had been halfway through a spam sandwich and her thoughts were still with it.

'Come on woman, snap to it! Time is of the essence. The beast is loose!'

◆ ◆ ◆

Initially, Uncle Otto, Willy and Horst had felt like the pit ponies whose pictures were so often displayed on the front pages of Welsh newspapers, as they were plucked from the depths of the pits and released into springtime fields for a few short weeks and ran and rolled and frisked in disbelief at sudden freedom in a wonderful world intoxicatingly rich in sights and tastes and textures. They never showed them as they were betrayed and dragged back to the hell of renewed slavery down in the deep mines. But the trio were disappointed in the world as revealed in the A48 that ran in front of the camp. It had let them down badly. They had observed the tantalising lights of slow-moving American trucks on so many nights, pausing at the junction and offering an ideal opportunity for scrambling aboard unseen. But tonight, for some reason, the road seemed deserted except for the odd private car that was best avoided. On his work forays beyond the wire, Willy had noticed an old Austin 10 – running boards and mudguards edged with splodges of white paint for the blackout – more or less permanently parked outside one of the bigger houses in a nearby residential street. Perhaps it would be there again tonight. They moved across the main road under the cover of the trees and, sure enough, there it was, a great dark lump, crouched and waiting at the kerbside.

The stethoscope left on ledge of the back window was the usual laissez-passer of a doctor so they could reasonably hope it would have privileged access to fuel and that might also help with any nosy official who wondered what they were doing out and about at that hour. The door lock and ignition yielded rapidly enough to Otto's technical expert tickling and soon Willy was at the wheel as the engine turned over, coughed once and died. They all cursed and Willy tried again. The noise was like thunder in the night time silence, echoing back from the blank walls, only to die again. The battery must be flat. They watched fearfully for a light coming on in the house, knowing, if it did, they would have to make a run for it on foot. And then they heard voices coming down the street.

Four soldiers, unarmed, all drunk, clearly on their way back from the pub to the camp, weaving along the pavement towards them. It was too late to just run. They would have to bluff it out. The troopers surrounded the car, still singing some dirty song about a mademoiselle of Armentières, their breath steaming in the frosty air.

'Having a bit of trouble? Isn't this Dr. Blair's car?'

Considering himself the only adult, Otto took the lead, leaning out of the window with a serious look on his face and a voice of clipped authority. 'The doctor is waiting for us at the hospital. We have to join him there. It is rather urgent and the car won't start.'

The squaddie straightened up. 'Well, sir, we'd better give you a shove then. Come on lads.'

They rallied round the back and put their shoulders into it. "One, two, three. Push!' Willy released the handbrake and the car set off rumbling down the road and soon they had picked up enough pace and Willy let out the clutch with a great Thunk! The old Austin lurched and skidded and the engine caught with a roar and they began to move forward in a cloud of blue smoke. One of the soldiers fell over laughing and the others cheered and waved their arms in farewell.

'Left! Willy! Drive on the left!'

◆ ◆ ◆

'This is the BBC Home Service. Here is the news for today, Sunday the eleventh of March, and this is Alvar Lidell reading it. Seventy Germans escaped from a prisoner of war camp at Bridgend, Glamorgan, last night. So far, twenty-three have

been recaptured. Hundreds of troops, police and civilians have been taking part in the search and it is thought that the men may have found cover in the Welsh hills, and sparsely-populated valleys or in the caves and sand dunes on the coast a few miles
from the camp. Many former Home Guards, living in the area, have volunteered to help in the search.'

◆ ◆ ◆

WPC Shawcross was hot and tired. Her fingers were all sticky with glue and sore from being pricked with pins. A policewoman's life was not a happy one. Superintendent May had not been in the least grateful when she finally handed in her cache of little flags in an old biscuit tin with a look of triumph on her face. In fact, he had tutted that the glue was not yet dry and some of the pins had stuck together. He could be such an old woman. For two pins...well never mind. He could stuff it up his Huntley and Palmers. She stumped back to her desk and sucked at her fingers.

Superintendent May crossed to the large map he had fixed to the wall and began to stick the little flags into the places where prisoners had been apprehended - like von Rundstedt moving up his tank divisions to defend the Atlantic Wall. He hesitated a moment, being tempted to put a great cluster of them at the camp itself to make the whole thing look a bit more encouraging but that would be cheating and ruin the arithmetic. That was what the BBC had done, counting those who had not got further than a few hundred yards from the camp as recaptured but not deducting them from the total declared as having got away in the first place. That was the sort of dishonest thing Hitler had done and that would lead to his downfall. But Superintendent May was made of sterner stuff and stuck to his first two, upright, honest, little flags in Llanharan. The chief danger was that prisoners would be recaptured and sent back without his being informed. That could lead to absolute chaos in his biscuit tin.

That joke he had made about sheep. It was the moment to take it seriously. He had seen to it that every preacher in every chapel was approached and told to pass on the need for the Christian virtue of vigilance to his flock. One rose to his feet that Sunday and favoured his congregation with a long sermon about how the Israelites were led out of captivity but, because of their sins, delivered back into the hands of their enemies and declared, 'The police have asked us to watch out for these murdering swine and cast them back into the pit of their own iniquity – which we shall do in the Christian spirit of forgiveness and divine mercy. Let us all stand and sing "Glorious Things of Thee Are Spoken", number 233 in your hymn books.' It was only when the first wheezy notes were played on the asthmatic harmonium that they realised it was the same tune as the German National anthem.

♦ ♦ ♦

Colonel William Llewellen, ex-Home Guard, fellow mason, sat proudly astride his horse and surveyed the sand dunes rather like his hero, Lawrence of Arabia astride a camel in the Empty Quarter. That his sand dunes were in windily Welsh Ogmore-on-Sea, not the blazing Levant, took nothing away from the comparison. The enemy was out there somewhere, skulking toerags in the arid wastes or hiding in the big caves down by the river mouth and they would flush them out by criss-crossing the allegedly uninhabited area. It wasn't helpful that, as part of the destruction of pleasurable local amenities, the shoreline had been dotted with defensive, concrete pillboxes that provided ideal shelter for dossers. The British War Office had been less generous to Llewellen than it had been to Lawrence, they had even taken his men's bicycles away and refused to issue a supplementary petrol ration to aid the search for the Bridgend escapees, though he had spent a furious morning on the telephone to anyone of influence he had ever met. Faced with universal stony unhelpfulness, he had taken matters into his own hands and mobilised the full force of the local hunt, though – to the disappointment of some - insisting that hunting pink should not be worn and no hounds should be present. That would have been a little too reminiscent of what the Jerries had got up to in South West Africa where they also had sand dunes, in the days of innocence when war was seen to be the same harmless pleasure as watching a fox being torn to pieces by frenzied dogs. On the other hand, one or two had precautionary shotguns which would have been very bad form on a foxhunt. He stood up in his stirrups, enjoying the sense of strain in his legs and the creak of well-tended leather and scanned along the skyline from the black rocks and the devil's bunting of beachside barbed wire, over to the Merthyrmawr Warren, sweeping his field glasses slowly and methodically over the terrain. Once the black Americans had been billeted here and their presence lingered on in a thin scatter of windblown, military litter, old ammunition boxes and cockeyed signs directing visitors to the PX, all a testament to the lavish waste of war. Despite the thin, cold breeze, the sun was bright and casting dense shadows that shifted with the clouds, making things difficult to distinguish. Wait. His arm paused and moved back. There was something there, a definite movement in the distance. He looked more carefully. There had been an embarrassing incident of seagulls being identified as parachutists that must not be repeated.

He pointed. 'There!' and turned. 'Hey, you! Stop that!'

One of the younger boys had raised a hunting horn to his grinning lips for a triumphant 'Tally-ho'. Llewellen, furious, wrenched round his mount's head and grabbed it from him, turned again and set off to lead them down a steep declivity and across a flat, watery stretch, breaking into a canter over the firm sand and up into the far dunes. The surf thundered in their ears as they crested a ridge and felt the stiff, cold wind from the sea blowing a fine spray of salted sand in their faces and there, beneath them, was a sort of nest, constructed in a deep hollow, of gorse branches and rough grass. Llewellen let out a cry of triumph. Then there came a series of metallic

clicks and men in tropical uniforms, sporting foliage-stuffed hats and minstrel-blackened faces rose up silently from the ground and covered them from all sides with rifles.

♦ ♦ ♦

Superintendent May had had a slow day. It had been hours before the telephone began to ring, bringing in news of fresh catches. After each call, he would carefully affix more pins to his wall map and then call Darling's ADC to arrange for the new haul to be picked up and taken back to Bridgend. Presumably a little jaunt to get off base and pick up some Jerries was now a hotly-contested perk for the disgraced guards. The escapees were to be penned up in the old theatre area and put on basic rations as the whole camp was turned over with what was doubtless the usual ruthless inefficiency. For Darling, the devil lay always in the military detail and he seemed much more keen to punish his own slack troops – who had done wrong - rather than the Germans – who had only done what was expected of them - and they were to be confined to barracks until further notice with a couple put on charges for rough handling of the recaptured. Rumours abounded of PoWs being made to run the gauntlet with a boot up the arse from Sergeant Wilson as the <u>coup de grâce</u> –'Careful you don't trip and hurt yourself now' - of being made to strip naked and sit bolt upright for hours until their muscles screamed, of lost teeth and bruised ribs, even of shots being fired over their heads. The British troops, who had their own rumour mill, were told in whispers that, to expiate their crimes, they were all bound for a suicidal attack on French North Africa where grinning Arabs were whetting long, curly knives, eager to be cutting their lily-white throats. Most of them would not have made it as far as the docks.

By now, there were a couple of dozen little flags waving bravely on Superintendent May's map, as on a miniature golf course, but still plenty more rattling around like unfulfilled dreams in the biscuit tin on his desk. He looked at the tin, stamped with colourful scenes from British country life, a farmer ploughing with freshly-combed shire horses, immaculate, leaping maypole dancers, a child stooping to pick daffodils in a sun-bathed woodland glade and thought of - biscuits – proper chocolate biscuits, crunchy, silky, unctuous, whose ghostly smell still haunted the tin. He bent forward and inhaled deeply of the breath of angels with closed eyes. To be honest, it was the biscuits he missed most, not the fled Arcadia that bore little resemblance to Glamorgan as he knew it. He pushed the flags to one side as the telephone shrilled out again, pressed his fingers to a few, lingering crumbs he spotted in one corner and raised them to his lips.

◆ ◆ ◆

'Hands up! Bang, bang!'

Not 'Peng, peng!' British troops then, not armed Germans or even mislaid black Americans. And sparing scarce ammunition in training. Relief swept over the huntsmen. An officer struggled up the sandy slope from the gulley below, red-faced and puffed up. Like the troops, he was absurdly dressed in shorts but with solar topee instead of steel helmet and blue with cold.

'Who the devil are you? We weren't told anything about cavalry. Don't you know better than to enter a military area when there's a training exercise going on? Didn't you see the warning flags for God's sake?' He looked them up and down and suddenly, deep in the recesses of his mind, a penny dropped. 'I say. You wouldn't be those Jerries we've been told to watch out for, would you?' His eyes narrowed and his hand moved towards his pistol.

The Colonel was dumbfounded. 'That's what we were about to ask you, dammit. Do I look or sound like a twenty-year-old SS officer to you?'

'Anything unusual is what we were told to watch out for,' he said sullenly. 'Now I'd say you look pretty unusual to me. In fact, you're the most unusual thing I've seen in weeks.'

'Same to you with knobs on. Khaki drill and tropical headgear is hardly proper dress for this climate. As Germans, you might well have stolen a batch of it and know no better. I think your activities could rightly be called suspicious.'

'Or just perhaps we could be battle-hardened troops doing final combat training before heading out East to take on the Japs.'

'Perhaps you could.'

'Right, then.'

'Right.'

They stared at each other, then burst out laughing, a tacit recognition that military preparedness was somehow deeply unBritish.

The men stood around, rifles drooping miserably, bare legs shaking and teeth chattering with cold, twiggy helmets feeling like a sack of coal on their heads and dreamed of mugs of hot tea as they gaped confusedly at this outbreak of public school solidarity from an alien world. Bloody officers. Haw-hawing at each other like a couple of laughing hyenas and they rapidly translated the experience into their own murmured subaltern terms. What a f-ing waste of our f-ing time. F-ing us about like f-. Crazy the whole f-ing lot of stupid f-ers.

On the way back, the hunt treated themselves to a good gallop on the hard sand by the water's edge, to give the horses something to do, before turning inland and literally stumbling over a hollow with three of the missing Germans huddled in it, having clearly just finished a scratch meal. The hunt were appalled by the Hogarthian scene before them - abandoned sardine tins, ashes, bottles, scraps of newspaper that had been used to wipe unmentionable things, walls striated with urine – all much worse than those East-Enders squatting in bomb-craters that were made so much of in the papers. They had obviously installed themselves here some time ago and been keeping a low profile till the search died down. The colonel looked down his long nose at them. His horse looked down its even longer nose and snorted at the rising miasma of rancid fish and stale humanity.

'I knew we'd find a use, sooner or later, for those blasted gas masks we've been carrying around for years,' opined the youngest huntsman to a general laugh. The colonel managed, at best, a wan smile. He knew, as they did not, that the masks they had been issued with would have been totally useless against any gas the Germans might have decided to drop.

And in the midst of it all a fourth man, oblivious to the intrusion, was whistling and continuing to polish his already immaculate boots with every sign of soldierly satisfaction.

'Good man that.' said the Colonel, approvingly.

♦ ♦ ♦

'This is a total cock-up, Henderson, a shitstorm, what our American cousins call a "cluster fuck".' The minister reached for a cigarette, then thought about the wearying complexity of the process he had embarked on, of finding matches, lighting the bloody thing, laying hands on the ashtray, smoking it and gave up in despair, abandoning the cigarette unlit on the desk. He just didn't have the strength any more. It was all too much. He'd eaten a martyr's lunch with some dire Labour MP from up north, a wandering piece of Housedruff, who had insisted on the British Restaurant. It had been some sort of inflatable steak and kidney pudding with organic slime at its core. Then had come the mauling in the Press and the Chamber.

'Yes, sir. Very expressive. What we might call, in our own argot, an embarrassment of embarrassments. Chums in the know say the PM is taking time off from being ecstatic about the whole of Europe to be furious about Wales and fair bouncing his false teeth off the walls of the Cabinet Office.'

'I suppose you got that from your girlfriend.'

The first rule of government was, of course, to always blame your civil servants but the minister had taught Henderson to begin all his correspondence, "The minister thanks you for your letter of the Xth inst. and has instructed me to reply to you as follows..." His personal responsibility would be trampled over every document, ignoring suggestions for improving security and requests for proper resources, putting off, cutting back – each one a nail in his coffin. The paper trail would lead any hunter back to his lair.

'I have it hot from the PM's desk, minister, or at least from his wastepaper basket.'

'You will not remember but Winnie is always a bit touchy about Wales since they hung that label round his neck, sending in troops to shoot at the striking miners in Tonypandy while he was Home Secretary. He still denies it, of course, but that's irrelevant. That's all people remember. How are we doing in Bridgend? How many recaptured? How many still on the loose?'

Henderson looked down at his notes and made a face. 'Slightly unclear. At the moment, it looks a bit like 39 to the Jerries and 31 to you, sir. Bit of a black eye, I'd say.'

The minister threw himself back in his chair and puffed. That switch from 'us' to 'you' had not gone unnoticed. The rats might not yet be leaving the sinking ship but they were building a gangplank for a swift and splashless departure at the first sign of a rising water level. 'Right. Now, remind me. How many of our chaps got out of the Stalag Luft III PoW camp last year?'

'I think the official number is still 70, minister.'

'So we're still beating the Jerries by 70 to 68 and they copied us in digging their way out. Hang on to that thought. And the 90-odd Eyties that got away from Doonfoot Camp before Christmas also knocked the Krauts into a cocked hat. That's number two. Number three. How are we doing in the late extras today? Have you had time to go through them?'

Henderson reached for a pile of newspapers stacked on the chair beside him. 'Could be worse, minister, as some have usefully got hold of the wrong end of the stick. The <u>Express</u> has hundreds of troops and Home Guard mobilised and armed with Tommy guns and spotter aircraft up in the skies within minutes of the escape.'

'Spotter planes? Good idea. Look into that. Even if they can't see Jerries, the people can still see <u>them</u> which stops them getting huffy and asking what we're doing. One of the lessons of Dunkirk.'

'And according to the tabloids, the escapees are apparently all devil-may-care, fanatical Nazis, strangling babies and stamping around in jackboots.'

'Well, that will keep people on their toes. Good thing, don't you think?'

'The <u>Herald</u> and the <u>Worker</u> have them "possibly armed", so at any minute we can expect people to start blazing away at each other in all directions at the slightest creak of a floorboard and there's other weird stuff about the Germans once being allowed to goosestep through the town market at the funeral of an inmate. Oh! and the cartoonists are having an absolute field day showing the camp as a sort of luxury spa hotel with fat Germans being waited on hand and foot by our men, scuttling about like waiters. Would you care to see? This one's frightfully clever.' He sniggered.

The minister buried his head in his hands and groaned. 'No. No.' He looked up, a small hope in his voice. 'No cartoon pictures of me, I expect.' He knew he had a face and body shape that he would be an easy gift to the cartoonist's cruel art. At school, he had been compared unfavourably to a penguin. He must stop wearing that pork pie hat that opened the door to too many cruel puns and rhyming slang. He remembered bitterly the story that had been put about when he was in the Ministry of Supply that, when the C-in-C Egypt requested 50,000 sandbags, he had shipped them from England ready-filled.

'Not yet, sir, but we can be sure they're sharpening up their pencils as we speak.'

The ministerial face hardened into action. 'Right. Number four. Get hold of that damned nephew of mine and tell him all filming at Bridgend is off. Say "security blackout". There'll have to be a board of enquiry right away.'

Henderson lowered the papers and raised his eyebrows. 'Isn't that a bit premature, minister? The escapees haven't even been rounded up yet.'

'Absolutely not. It will look as if we're grasping the nettle and, if we act sharpish, we can quickly decide who goes on the board before the jackals in the House start getting organised and move in on the carcass. But we have to be quick off the mark. The man who controls the past, controls the future.'

'But what if they don't come to the right conclusion? They might dig up some rather embarrassing memos from this office.' He tapped on his tongue with his pencil as if signifying his own ability to blab.

Henderson, he reminded himself, was very young. 'Unlikely, since we appoint the board and hand out a few grateful medals at the end of the process. Nothing like a great big gong to keep things quiet. If, by some stretch of the imagination, that happens, then we declare the report classified on security grounds and assure those buggers of the Presstapo that recommendations on procedures, improvements etc. have already been reviewed and implemented so that criticisms no longer apply. Questions have been boldly asked and clearly answered in a manner that is a tribute to our democratic system of government that speaks truth unto power so they can just keep their bloody traps shut. In the long run, young man, there are only two ways to deal with a cock-up on this scale. Either everyone gets a boot up the arse or they get promoted with a gong and a housepoint. In my experience, the second is always by far the easier and the preferred choice of a true statesman. Virtue is its own reward because that's usually the only reward it gets.'

'Er...won't people think that's a bit of a whitewash?'

The minister sat back and laughed at the innocence of youth. Henderson showed himself up at times as the whippersnapper he was. He felt a resurgence of mature confidence and flexed his arms. 'With the big victory coming and the return of our own troops, people aren't going to be too bothered about any of this, Henderson. The public memory is very short. We just have to make it that far and they will be falling over themselves to pass the parcel and shout about the need to get rid of the PoWs and shuffle them off our rations as soon as possible. The whole fiasco will be a dead duck if not a dead dodo. Anyway, who ever heard of an army camp that didn't use whole bucketloads of whitewash?'

He felt the glow of comfort and pleasure that comes from having reduced a particular case to a general principle and sat back smiling in his chair. 'Time for a dish of tea and a sticky bun, I think. Do you think you could organise that, Henderson?'

◆ ◆ ◆

CHAPTER SEVEN

Superintendent May peered at the Ordnance Survey map spread over his wall with boyish curiosity. It was quite extraordinary the things you saw on the official map of a place you thought you knew so well by just walking over it – railway cuttings, little lakes he didn't know were there because they were hidden in the trees, disused mines – a whole secret world unavailable to the everyday senses. He strained to read a hidden meaning in the pattern of dotted flags as if they were a message in Braille but the only truth he extracted was that they were like a joyless ring doughnut without jam, with the camp at its empty centre.

They had been lucky thus far. None of the prisoners had resisted but surrendered like lambs. A bold, young ATS girl had spotted a pair on a country lane and just walked up and grabbed them by the scruff of the neck and frogmarched them off to the police station as a headmistress might two naughty fourth formers playing truant. When the men were searched this time, they only had a sort of spicy, dried toast in their pockets. Perhaps that was what Germans ate, a bit like hamsters. It was clear the SS had taken charge of the best stolen food for their own use and left the others pretty much to live off the land which offered slim pickings at this time of year. In other words, the others were being used as a mere tactical diversion for SS escapers. As townies, they mostly hadn't a clue anyway, so that they were pretty down in the mouth when recaptured.

The RAF had had lots of fun swooping around in their spotter planes and worrying and stampeding the sheep off hillsides better than any rabid dogs might have done but since they could only communicate with their own control tower by radio, who could only communicate with May by telephone, who could only communicate with police officers when they themselves went into a telephone box to call in, they didn't really help much. And there were endless aggrieved officers who had been obliged to pay tuppence for the calls out of their own pocket when the bickering operator refused to put them through without charge. By the time their information reached the men on the ground and officers had raced to the spot on their bicycles, the escapees might have taken a quick nap before casually strolling off. The airmen were only useful on foot to bulk up other forces.

Nevertheless, more and more prisoners were now being pinned to the map and ever fewer still rattled around in the Arcadian biscuit tin. Near Southampton, a lady tracked some down with her pet bloodhound. Two more were enticed from hiding by the smell of a troop of Girl Guides, or rather by the smell of their frying rissoles on a field trip. More were detected on a bus of miners with theatrically blackened faces like banjo-playing Al Jolson that fooled no one. The public viewed the agents of officialdom with some suspicion, having encountered them mainly in the form of billeting officers who tried to force loathsome slum children into their homes and confiscatory agricultural officers who poked their unwelcome noses into their cowsheds and sheep pens, but they had joined in the manhunt enthusiastically. One determined participant even set fire to a whole mountain in shifting wind and thus – unfortunately – his own house to flush out anyone hiding there in the undergrowth. Elsewhere, two timorous ladies on an isolated farm – fearful of being sexually enjoyed by whole troops of lusty, blond beasts - laid out a neat plateful of sandwiches on the window sill every night to keep the forces of darkness away and scattered sand underneath to make sure it wasn't the fairies. The next morning they saw that, if it was fairies, then they were very hungry fairies that wore great big boots.

May was often surprised by the reactions of people to war news. When there had been an early scare about parachutists, he had heard one woman remark, 'Parachutists? That's good. I could use some new silk drawers.' He had been impressed and by the way the PoWs were treated by the Welsh populace, especially now that news of the horrors of the concentration camps and the pictures of starving, Allied prisoners in German hands were on every cinema screen. The answer to the presence of escaped prisoners was, almost universally, not a good hiding but a cup of tea, an apologetic spam sandwich and a place by the fire. The only exception, to which a blind eye would be turned, was a sweet-faced SS officer whose extreme youth roused pity in the heart of a farmer's wife as he sat, glumly waiting to be picked up on a remote farm. She gave him a cup of tea that he poured sneeringly on the ground, so her husband took him outside and gave him a right thumping to teach him respect for human compassion. It was important to keep things cool, to avoid inflaming emotions, to reduce the search to neat, calm paperwork. Of course, accidents would still happen. A couple more PoWs had suffered unwitting insult by tiptoeing into town at closing time and ducking into a ditch across the way from the pub as the door was suddenly flung open and the careless drinkers spilled out into the street in a square of light. The patrons staggered across the road, blind in the darkness, shouting their goodbyes and relieved themselves extravagantly in some outpouring rite of male solidarity in the ditch and all over the crouching escapees.

◆ ◆ ◆

The tension of the manhunt produced its moments of high drama. Smasher Wilkins, a sharp-eyed reporter from <u>The News of The World</u>, was hard at work, labouring through his expenses allowance in the bar of the Metropolitan Hotel in Swansea, writing up background stuff and wondering if he might find copyworthy sleaze amongst the mackintosh trade of the whorehouses over in Tiger Bay, when a suspicious pair over in one corner caught his eye. Young men, not in uniform, hanging about in public during working hours were always up to no good. One was big-boned, blond and blue-eyed, a typical Nazi type, and both were wearing long, navy-blue overcoats and giveaway heavy, black boots of identical design. Even their hats looked as if they had come from the same department store. He pricked up his ears and slid from the bar, casually wandering past their table as if a confused stranger looking for the gents and caught a trace of guttural conversation in a foreign tongue before they noticed him and immediately fell silent and watchful. On the table lay a copy of the Irish ferry timetable and a plate with two evil-looking sausages. One pretended to slice at a sausage with his knife so he could slide his arm furtively over the schedule. Smasher's heart leapt. This was it! His big scoop! It was what he had dreamed of for years in a life spent haunting village fêtes and then divorce courts, struggling vainly to inject excitement into distended sheep and stained sheets. He could see it all. The gnomic little old man who wrote headlines had a special skill for devising deliciously ambiguous front pages. His had been the famous 'Hitler Has Only Got One Goal – Official', 'French Push Bottles Up Ten Thousand Germans!' and 'Docklands Air Raid: RAF Shoot Down Sixteen Big Fokkers'. Perhaps it might be 'Smasher Nails Two Camp Nazis'. His smiling picture looking modest as byline as he wrestles them to the ground. No wait. This was a pair of big lads, trained killers. Maybe best to just telephone the police and let them deal with it. 'Smasher's Red-Hot Tip Gets A Result'. He panted across the chipped marble tiles of the hallway to the telephone booth and dialled 999 with trembling finger. 'Two foreigners - obvious Nazi types - speaking German - looking at Shipping Report', then returned to the bar and climbed back on his stool, pencil poised, to witness the arrests. A few minutes later the police arrived in the form of two flustered constables. He winked at them and waggled his finger discreetly at the corner table and watched in the mirror over the bar as they reached for their truncheons and prepared to close in. They peered across the room, shook their heads, went over and the men looked up and exchanged a few words and stared across at him, leaned forward looking puzzled and then gave a bark of laughter as they lay down their knives, mouths full of chewed sausage.

'Two of our own plain clothes officers, sir. Did you think you'd spotted a pair of U-boat captains, then? Oh, and by the way, that German they was speaking was something we call Welsh. You may have heard of it.'

They walked away sniggering. Never mind. After a couple more drinks, Smasher's inspiration had ripened journalistically. The brain that had transformed every puff of wind into a hurricane, every bloodied German nose into a triumphant Allied massacre, every shot fired into a fusillade would not fail him now. The Germans were supposed to have tried to release a load of submariners from Canadian incarceration the year before and whisk them away in a U-boat. He stirred that into the mix churning in his brain and gave the lurking, plainclothes bobbies a bashful thumbs-up - 'Our reporter made an excuse and left' - and swayed back to the telephone booth with a stack of pennies to dial up the copy editor in London and dictate the afternoon's events down the line - 'Panic flares in Swansea - desperate police raid in city centre on knife-wielding suspects following secret tip-off – in official circles rumours persist of U-boats detected cruising off the coast ready to land and carry away hardened Nazis.'

♦ ♦ ♦

Billy and his gang thrilled to the news of the escape. Unlike their parents, they had been depressed by the realisation that the war would soon be over and before they were old enough to lay hands on a glamorous army uniform made out of flour sacks and take part in it. Admittedly, the boys had done their best to do their bit. There was the time they had found an unexploded anti-aircraft shell and Billy had proudly brought it home, gleaming with brassy menace. The story had been published in the local newspaper under the single-word headline 'Imprudence!' He thought of it as 'Ingratitude!' And it had to be admitted that the Home Guard with its bumbling old farts and wooden rifles had taken the gilt off the military gingerbread. But now an adventure was delivered on their very doorstep, something worthy of Enid Blyton's Five. Ignoring parental attempts to keep them inside, they roamed the countryside on their bicycles, armed with stout sticks, secure in the young certainty of their own immortality. To ensure their anonymity during operations, they disguised themselves with burnt cork moustaches and padded out their cheeks with chewed newspaper.

'But what do we do, if we find any Jerries?' Fred paled. He was a thin child, always the most nervous, but then his dad had actually died after finding quite a lot of Jerries in North Africa.

'Citizen's arrest. Then they have to come with us and we march them off to the nick. That's the law.'

'Why the nick? We should take them back to the camp. I reckon we'd get a reward if we did that.' Of course, Arthur's own dad had been marched off to the nick, if rumour was to be believed, and there had been no reward flowing from that.

'Let's not count our eggs before they're hatched.' Jimmy's dad, the preacher, was a master of homespun rhetoric and had passed on the gift to his son.

An odd crunching noise came from down the hill. They leapt up and were delighted to see a squad of odd-looking soldiers, marching along and swinging their arms in a jaunty, rather unmilitary, fashion – not the hoped-for SS but, by the look of them, FFs, Free French. They were popular enough around the town. Billy loved the smell of them – dark tobacco, garlic, red wine - but his grownup sister had gathered her cardie about her bosom in that unambiguous female gesture of complaint and joked that the trouble with them was that they were a bit too free with their free-frenching. They were led by some sort of officer with magnificent moustaches and curly gold braid on his sleeves and were happily singing that popular song from the wireless, the one sung by that Red Indian girl, Kay Starr, with big grins on their faces.

"Come out, come out wherever you are
I know, I know you're not very far!
How I wish you'd hurry
'Cause I'm inclined to worry;
These arms of mine are open
Hoping you'll appear
Where are you, dear?"

The boys ran down the slope, abandoning their bicycles, and attached themselves delightedly to the tail end of the column and thought themselves rather better at marching than these FFs and certainly better singers than these voices that were soaked in snails and frogs' legs.

"Come out, come out wherever you are
Come out, come out from under that star!
Yes, and incidentally
Mentally
I'm not up to par
So come out, come out, come out
Wherever you are."

It was a delirious day. The captain, for such he was revealed to be, took their burnt cork moustaches as some sort of homage to his own facial hair and the honour of France. When the troops paused to refresh themselves at a pub, a glass of lemonade and a bag of crisps were sent out to them, acknowledging them as part of the troop. To them it was as priceless champagne and <u>foie gras</u>. Billy instructed his men to ignore the blue twist of 'salt' inside the bag. Everyone knew it was some chemical put there by the government to make men's todgers go limp so they would put all their

energy into the war effort. And then they were allowed to lead the whole squad, glowing with pride, to some nearby ruins that were to be searched.

◆ ◆ ◆

CHAPTER EIGHT

The reporters were finding it hard going. Keeping up a supply of trivial news for the ever-demanding London papers was straining the powers of invention of even seasoned factual reporters. Smasher's scoop had been greeted with unmixed jealousy by his colleagues. They were heartily sick of peaceful sheep and plucky Dunkirk spirit and unspoilt villages that had survived centuries of change unscathed and where time had trickled by as gently as the streams of the valleys. Irate editors were clamouring for anything that could be used to beat the government with. They had been delighted to find confirmation that PoWs received better rations than the British civilians who - gripped in the midst of a worldwide meat shortage - were now hungry for more outrage. Tales of bacchanalian goings-on at the camp had been teased painstakingly out of unwilling witnesses - everything from excess singing - doubtless fuelled by drink - to the scandalous waste of good food in the swill bins of men living high on the hog - only to be quashed by swiftly-imposed D-notices. And then, in the quiet, midnight streets of Porthcawl, a single shot rang out that echoed the length of Fleet Street.

Porthcawl had its share of the human violence that was normal part of social life, drunken brawls relating to football, domestic discussions that got out of hand, disagreements involving politics or the Eisteddfodau but they never ended up in gunplay. At the most, there were broken skulls and black eyes. Witnesses who ran to the scene that wet and windy night found two huddled figures on the slick pavement. Mrs. Lilly Grossley lay sprawled in the gutter with her husband, Howard, bent over her.

'It was a German! 'he cried between sobs. 'Two Germans. They've shot my wife!'

'Germans', Lilly confirmed hoarsely, as they loaded her into the ambulance. 'They tried to snatch my handbag – the good one from Timothy White's with the clasp fitting that looks like gold - and then they run off.'

She was taken to the hospital with a serious chest wound that might yet prove fatal but with her thoughts more fixed on the irreparable damage to her best overcoat. Her husband was understandably distraught.

This was the worst possible thing that could have happened, as far as Superintendent May was concerned. Immediately, he translated it in his mind into wild headlines, violent incidents, panicked troops gunning down unarmed prisoners, farmers letting off their shotguns at anything that moved. He imposed a total news blackout but in the sad foreknowledge that leaks were impossible to avoid, he called a press conference.

May looked out over a bobbing sea of fag-puffing little men all wearing the trademark clothes of the reporter, trilby hats and trenchcoats, all shouting, nobody listening, like in an Irish parliament.

'Good morning, gentlemen.'

At the sound of his voice, the hubbub dimmed in shock – they were not being used to being called gentlemen - and subsided into a rustle of notepads and licked pencils. Before the packed room, he briefly outlined the events of the previous night as any decent constable would in a magistrate's court – calmly and dispassionately, stripping away the tangled human emotions that alone made human actions intelligible, so that they seemed to hang suspended in the air like the acts of ghosts. He urged that any connection with the escaped prisoners was totally unproven. Picking up on old slogans that still resounded in the public mind, he hammered home the terrible consequences of any loose talk, the fact that it would play into enemy hands and – like a Christian missionary before a heathen tribe - held out the promise of full disclosure of all his secrets on the morrow in return for silence today. Anyone letting the cat out of the bag would be excluded from all further briefings. The reporters went into a cluster. It was a matter of group solidarity over personal rivalry, insecurity over ambition, the smell of the sort of scoop that justified a hundred nights of grubby hotels, coffee that tasted of fag-ash and food not fit for a dog. Incredibly, hope triumphed over experience and Superintendent May had bought himself a whole day before the wires to Fleet Street would run red hot.

Back in his command HQ, the superintendent lay aside his well-thumbed biscuit tin and reverted to being an old-fashioned copper. He carefully read up on what his men had already established as the background to the case and strongly smelled a rat. Nose-twitching, he put on his hat, picked up his swagger stick and set off for the local police station to interview Howard Grossley, himself.

First, it turned out from what he had read, that the woman involved was not Mrs. Grossley at all. Her true identity was Lily Griffiths, unmarried, and the pair had a child, the illegitimate, sole result of four years' vigorous cohabitation - therefore in local speech she was damned as 'no better than she should be' and her every word subject to doubt. Her 'husband', Howard Grossley, was actually a Canadian trooper who had gone AWOL. He had a foul temper and a history of drunken violence and was regarded around the town as a man to be avoided. Grossley was allegedly often doped up to the eyebrows on painkillers following severe injuries, mysterious but extensive burns, that he claimed made him unfit for further service. He often carried a single-stack service automatic. When he heard of the PoW escapes, he had sent the lad of the house upstairs to fetch it, loaded it before his terrified eyes and waved it about, threatening to shoot any Jerries he encountered.

The whole situation offended much more than just the chapel-going starch in Superintendent May's collar. Initially, the soldier had confessed to having shot his 'wife' and his 'wife' had said he had shot her by mistake when they were attacked by a German. So at least it wasn't the German - who seemed to have disappeared into thin air - that was armed, a point to be stressed at tomorrow's Press conference. The doctor examining Lily noted extensive bruising to her face and arms and signs that she had been held and kicked in the abdomen – not totally unprecedented signs accompanying matrimonial affection in a mining community. The whole affair was more than fishy, it stank to high heaven.

Under the fluorescent lights of the chill, grimy interview room, May listened to Grossley's story with mounting scepticism though the man had clearly gone through the business in his mind and at least decided on a final, authoritative, King James, version. Unfortunately, this account did not hold water either but leaked in half a dozen places. The bullet fired had since been found in the wall of a nearby house. Forensic tests showed it matched Grossley's gun and the direction of fire completely contradicted his story. No trace had been found of any Germans in the area. Faced with skepticism, Grossley had retreated into truculence and crouched in a corner, dark and troglodytic. The burns that covered his lower body peeped out from under his collar.

'That's my story and I'm sticking to it,' he affirmed with arms folded. The human despair of a wretched, pointless life of self-hatred and poverty hung over the room like battlefield smoke.

It was time to use an old policeman's trick. May knew that Grossley might well have rehearsed the events in his mind but would not have internalised the accompanying actions. He asked him to step out into the corridor and re-enact the crime. Grossley was clueless, flummoxed, gestured wildly, broke down and confessed.

That night, a grim scene was enacted at the hospital where Lily lay on a chipped, enamel bed, having already been told she was dying. By the time Superintendent May arrived, Lily had undergone an operation and her bruises had had time to mature. One eye was closed and her whole body bore signs of extreme violence. It was hard to reconcile this image with the pretty, young woman described by all who knew her. The bullet had damaged her breast, lung and stomach, causing extensive trauma, infection and internal bleeding. Her organs were closing down, one by one. She had also been pregnant but the child had been aborted.

Around her bed, clustered shadowy figures in funereal blacks and blues - May, two Justices of the Peace, a solicitor, and at the back – sworn to silence – a handcuffed Howard Grossley. Lily took an oath that she would tell the truth, the whole truth and nothing but the truth in what was a legal dying declaration. Her previous statement, swearing that the shooting had been accidental and suffered while fending off a rabid German, was read to her and she confirmed its validity and declined to add anything except, 'Howard would never hurt me.' Superintendent May shook his head at the forgiving nature of women and thought of his mam.

Then a constable read out Howard's own recent statement in one of those doom-laden, 'I was proceeding in a northerly direction when...' voices that totally contradicted hers and she began to cry, the tears shaking her racked body. It now seemed that there had been no German after all, no attempted robbery. Her drunken lover had tried to shoot himself in an act of terminal despair not unusual at the time. They had wrestled over the gun and she had been the one shot. She managed to sign the new statement confirming this tale too with trembling fingers and passed away within days. Despite all this, a clear-sighted Glamorgan jury, disapproving of the marital irregularities of the case, was not to be misled by mere evidence and came to quite other conclusions, so that Howard Grossley would be unanimously found guilty of Lily's deliberate murder, led to the gallows and hanged with admirable despatch and demonstrations of righteous indignation outside the prison.

◆ ◆ ◆

'We have one great advantage...,' said Superintendent May, happily back in front of his map with a snappy folding pointer and an audience of his fellows - a public relations disaster successfully avoided. The newspaper men had all scuttled off to their telephones and rattled off their stories to editors who had twisted them to fit their various concerns. Grossley had only carried his gun, it was stressed by some, out of fear of the escapees, so it was still the Germans who were really responsible for the incident. Others had concentrated on hounding the sickly, illegitimate child, tucked away with an aunt, and using her as a terrible example of the complete moral collapse caused by the war.

'...It seems the PoWs were briefed by their leaders that all open water sources have been deliberately poisoned by the British authorities as a wartime security measure. They will not drink from streams or lakes or rivers or wells, so these men are going to be pretty thirsty and desperate for water.' In rainy Glamorgan, they would be like camels in the desert.

'So we should put an armed guard on every tap, is it?' An inspector from one of the outlying districts, passed over twice for promotion, who knew he would now rise no higher and had decided to make the most of it, saying all the delightfully unhelpful things he would have previously thought but left unspoken.

May sighed. He wasn't getting much sleep. There had been a major panic last evening when a cheery group of German orderlies, on their way to Bridgend to serve as batmen for the officers now absent and therefore needing no orderlies, had been nearly shot at the railway station. Others had ended up at the Ordnance Factory and caused a major flap, there not to execute some dire act of sabotage, but because almost all buses whisked you off there, whether you were willing or not, so that it was hard to go anywhere else around the town.

'No, but we should keep an eye on public sources of water, fountains and such in parks.'

Nearly a week had elapsed and there were sixty-odd brave little flags stuck on the map with almost all caught within a few miles of the camp. He had noticed that, as the tin gradually emptied, when he rattled it, the pitch of the noise it made rose accordingly, as if it were reflecting his own mounting state of stress and frustration.

'So why is it, sir, according to London, there were seventy escapees last week and only sixty-seven this? And if you include those recaptured nearby the camp itself there were eighty-four though you now say eighty-one?'

Superintendent May flushed red. 'Er...You must realise, inspector, it's all a matter of definition, at what point a prisoner may be said to have actually effected an escape.'

The inspector made a pop-eyed expression and stared round the room, mouth agape. 'Oh! Matter of definition is it?' Hand to heart in apology. 'And there was silly me thinking it was a matter of fact. Now, perhaps you can tell me, then, when one is recaptured, would that be a matter of definition or a matter of fact?'

Derisive laughter howled in May's ears.

◆ ◆ ◆

'Admit it, Willy, we're lost.' It seemed that in wartime Britain even medical doctors only had limited fuel and they could simply not afford to drive around in the dark like this. They had a little money from selling their wristwatches and chocolate rations to the guards and probably doctors had some special sort of official allowance book but a search of the car had revealed nothing so they could not buy more petrol. And now, surely this was the showy delights of central Cardiff - the anti-blast brown tape gummed over the windows being allowed to peel off by natural attrition and the fine, old railings cut down to rusty stumps and carried away to make cheap barbed wire - coming round for the third time? One bleak street looked much like another in the dim glowworm illumination of the headlights. The blackout had been relaxed now that further bombing was theoretically impossible, but at night the cities still looked as if they had been abandoned to lost dogs and questing cats. The plan had been to head inland towards Birmingham, not in this direction at all and not what the British would expect, and pick on one of the numerous airfields clustered together there. Soon, surely, the alarm would be raised back at the camp and there would be roadblocks everywhere. They had switched number plates with another car parked outside a locked garage some miles back but must get off the streets before then.

'We must head north-east.' Willy desperately tried to read a ripped-off shirttail in the gloom. 'Oh hell! I'm going to stop and ask.'

At first, there was simply no one to ask, then they spotted what looked like a workman from his coarse clothes striding out in the same direction and drew cautiously alongside, wound down the juddering window.

'Please can you tell us the way to Glowsester?'

He pulled up short. 'You what?'

'Glowsester? Please we are looking for Glowsester.' Willy's foot was on the accelerator, ready to speed away if things turned out that way.

The man stared, puzzled, then laughed as the penny dropped. 'You're not from round here are you?' They stiffened. Willy flexed his accelerator ankle and started rubbing the palm of his hand with the other thumb. It was suddenly throbbing unbearably. 'I think you must mean Gloucester.'

Willy laughed back. 'Gloster?' So the English confused people not just with no signs but also by their illogical spelling. 'Ah, so. No, we are Norwegian engineers, trying to find our way.'

'Well, you lads are miles out. In fact, you're halfway to "Old Cwembrahn".' They looked blank. 'Cwmbran? No? Never mind. Look, shove over and you can give me a lift and I'll point you in the right direction.' He slid onto the old cracked leather of the back seat with his tin lunchbox on his knees and exuded geographical confidence. 'Take the next left, now.'

They worried that their English might not be able to sustain an amicable conversation without giving themselves away but hardly a word was necessary. For several miles as the town fell away behind them, the passenger barely stopped talking. After a long diatribe expressing his resentment at the commandeering of his racing pigeons by the military authorities, he explored a seam of embarrassingly frank material to which there was no clear reply. 'My wife is a good woman, 'he revealed, 'but she is demanding and has sweaty thighs.' The extraordinary monologue lasted so long that they began to suspect that this man was cynically leading them far out of their planned route just to enjoy the benefits of a ride home and an unburdening conversation. From his relaxed demeanour, it was clear no escape alarm had reached him as yet. They eventually parted with cheery waves and firm directions – 'Mustn't make a noise now, or she'll be on me again' he whispered – and they watched him push through a gate plausibly enough so perhaps they were mistaken but it was inevitable now that they would run out of petrol out in the dark, blank and signless countryside before daylight.

When the old car began to splutter and cough like an outraged duchess, Willy steered them off the road and behind a tall hedge, gliding to a stop under some trees on squeaking leaf springs and barely avoiding hitting a tree that seemed to rise up out of nowhere. Perhaps it was the intimate conversation with their guide but it popped into his mind that Otto had told him that the Austrian buffoon, Dr. Freud, had declared that there was no such thing as an accident – but then they had never made Dr. Freud drive a car. The engine died into profound silence. Hiding it would give them a little more time before the abandoned vehicle was found. Horst insisted on leaving a note on the windscreen, apologising to the doctor for the theft and offering to pay for the petrol. He clearly had a more exalted view of the medical profession than Willy. And now they were on foot and the Forest of Dean beckoned to them in their outlawry as irresistibly as Sherwood had to Robin Hood.

The English greenwood was not at all the sort of thing they were familiar with – plushly budding and soon to be overleafed, including big, fat, deciduous trees not just the close-packed, misty firs of northern forests and with lots of undergrowth that the pine needles would have suffocated in their disinfectant smell. The best part was the ferns that offered cover and a soft bed as they wandered deeper into the woodland. Robin Hood would have fared much worse north of Hamburg. Once or twice, they even spotted a deer, an animal they previously only knew in the form of dark red sausages, but had no means to hunt them and no knowledge of how to deal with a dead one anyway since the gap between carcass and sausage was too great. Also, there was no rich harvest of nuts and berries to be gleaned, nothing accessible to eat at this time of winter sharpness, except the hard tack they had brought with them.

Around the edges of the treeline were nestling farms that should have offered up rich pickings. They tried to milk the cattle but just couldn't get the hang of it. Udders seemed unexpectedly complicated things and the cows turned and sneered at them before moving haughtily away like powerful locomotives with steaming breath. Henhouses were another promising source of easy food but whenever they set foot in one at night, the chickens would screech fit to raise the dead so that they always ended up just grabbing a couple of raw eggs and fleeing dogs and shotgun-wielding farmers who took them for foxes.

A needling rain had set in that depressed their spirits so that sleep came grudgingly and they woke, every morning, cold and stiff and shivery, longing for the familiar comforts of a heated concrete hut. They chain-smoked to keep hunger at bay and walked steadily north-east, keeping to the cover of the trees as much as possible. Then, on the third day, they heard a sound borne on the wind that lifted them more than church bells. It was the unmistakeable whine and roar of military aircraft taking off and landing. Willy pricked up his ears like a hunting dog with the smell of game in its nostrils. To him, it was a friendly sound.

'That's a Merlin engine. I'd know it anywhere.' He listened again, eyes shining, ear cocked. 'Hear that slight gurgle?' He held up a finger. 'That's the improved Bendix-Stromberg pressure carburettor that prevents fuel starvation when the plane is angled downwards. We all knew that was a design problem with the old Spitfires, so if you could force them into a steep dive...' He illustrated one with the flat of his hand. '... the engine would cut out and it was like child's play to shoot them down!' He breathed in through flared nostrils like an oenophile inhaling over a glass of complicated, vintage Bordeaux and tickling out the finer resonances. 'There are rumours that, with a new fuel additive, the latest Merlins produce a top speed that allows the RAF to even intercept the V1 ram-jet.' They stared at him blankly, having no idea what he was blathering about. It was time for a synopsis in their own language. He slapped Otto on the shoulder. 'We're going home, lads, courtesy of Rolls Royce!'

There was no information on the area to be gained from Otto's shirttail map.

'I shall execute a low-level recce,' Willy decided, nodding, eyes gleaming, glad to be professionally busy again. 'First I must become a Dutch flying officer once more. So I must make myself tall and polite – also clean.'

This involved going down to the icy stream that trickled through the little valley and plunging into it, gasping against the cold and the sharp stones underfoot. They had no mirror so Horst had to shave him, using the last of the bare razor-blades from the homemade compasses and the last fragment of soap to scrape off several days' beard. They dressed him up in the most respectable of their joint overcoats, gave him all their money and sent him off like a scrubbed schoolboy to class while they retreated into the thick ferns until he should return, Horst sucking at his blade-lacerated fingers.

◆ ◆ ◆

There was pale sunshine enough being filtered through the dappling trees to suggest spring and renewal though the same weather in Germany would only be encouraging the foreign tanks, spouting death and churning towards besieged

Berlin, their tracks ripping up the earth as they went. A few of the more optimistic birds were already singing a song of the eternal self-renewal of Nature after the passage of Man. One perched on a tree and looked at him, its beak full of twigs to begin the enormous task of post-war reconstruction and, in the distance, a cuckoo was imitating a Black Forest clock. The Black Forest where the Bulge had now been squeezed out like a pus-filled pimple. At school, they had had to sit through a lecture by a ranting Hitler Youth leader, with diagrams, about the Black Forest being the true home of the cuckoo clock, an original German design that had been stolen by the money-grubbing, racially-impure Swiss. His widowed mother had one over the stove on the kitchen wall at home, blithely unaware that it was an insult to the glorious Germanic peoples and the unfolding of their implacable destiny. Times of politics and argument everywhere. Yet, on a day like this, it was hard for Willy not to feel a little bit happy just to be simply alive though the memory of his mother was like a pressed flower, both sweet and sad. He put his hands on his waist, threw back his head and shouted, 'Cuckoo!'

He stepped out of the trees into soft, green hills and it was as if a blind were suddenly rolled up from over a window and stark light flooded down. He felt like Parsifal, dressed by his mother in a fool's clothes for his own protection, embarking on the spiritual quest for the Holy Grail at the court of King Arthur. They had learned that at school too. Someone called Wagner had even written an opera about it – there was an ending with something about a hovering white dove that had shat on the conductor at one performance and been in all the papers and made his father laugh. They had even put Parsifal on a stamp, holding a great cup like a goulash dish in both hands and with a haircut like Marlene Dietrich before she turned traitor. The word sizzled in his brain. According to mother, his father was supposed to have been knocked down by a tram in a traffic accident but a boy at school had whispered that both their fathers had been on the wrong side in one of the endless street demonstrations at the time that fell foul of the Brownshirts and their fists and wooden clubs. Willy had denied it, of course, and punched the boy almost senseless. At the thought, his burned hand began to hurt again.

A distant buzzing. He looked up to see a tiny, gnat-like aeroplane floating down purposefully over the next hill – a Hurricane – splayed wheels lowered for landing, the Merlin engine farting black smoke then powering up again out of sight. Hurricanes – despite their name - were relatively slow through the air but redeemed themselves by their ability to outturn anything in the sky and it was one of them that had shot down his Messerschmitt over Brest by going into a corkscrew dive and coming up behind him with its supercharger at full blast. It was an absurd and inglorious way to end up, like having a fat, white dove shitting on your head. The ache in his hand grew worse.

He moved slowly through the awakening countryside with its friendly, chaotic, animal and human noises of pottering and feeding – with none of the military overtones of the camp – deliciously alone and self-contained and the pain began to ease. Only now did it occur to him that a smiling Dutch pilot was still rather an odd thing to be found wandering about in remote English country lanes and might attract unwelcome attention but somehow there was a golden magic in the air. He was certain he had strolled into an illustration from a children's book, all in primary colours, where lark-filled skies were framed in lush rainbows without the need for rain, the sunlit air was cooled by the gentle flap of butterflies' wings and he knew himself quietly invisible in a landscape without nations.

♦ ♦ ♦

CHAPTER NINE

"It was better than we could ever have hoped for.' Willy had returned elated, wild-haired, pop-eyed from the strange and forgotten outside world that contained women who were not dyed weird colours and children, friendly dogs, flowers and lights you could turn on and off yourself. But it was also a world where everything was foreign and confusing – the colour of tickets, the shape of plugs, the functioning of door handles and locks. He had come back, a moth that had flown through the flame, after all kinds of insane adventures - bus rides, a visit to a pub, a conversation with a fuddled and unintelligible Scottish sailor who had bought him a drink but turned out to be rather more friendly than was strictly necessary, above all the discovery of an air base. And not just an air base – one with an attached flying school with low security. And now they were peering through the wire fence on a foggy, dew-soaked early morning, their whole bodies tingling with excitement.

'You see. Over that side is the RAF proper – Spitfires, Hurricanes' – the name Hurricane still made him wince, a nerve saw. 'Obviously, they would be the better option, faster, armed, longer range but see the sentries double-checking identity papers before anyone gets into that area and you can never tell whether the machines are fuelled up until you initiate startup procedures. Von Werra should never have written that booklet on how easy it is to steal a British fighter plane and escape. The Tommies learned from it.

But over this side, there's what is still almost a civilian flying school. And look at the pupils going through the gate. Uniforms of mixed nationalities, different languages, minimal attention paid to security if you get into a group. It's perfect!'

Otto gazed on them like Moses onto the promised land and shook his head sadly knowing he could not enter. 'It won't work. Look at them.' He pouted wearily. 'I'm too old. I stick out like an elephant in a flock of sheep. Anyway, trainer aircraft are two-seaters. You two try it. I'll stay behind or I'll just ruin your chances.' He turned away.

Horst and Willy were aghast. 'No! We've come this far together. Uncle! Look, pull your cap down, turn your collar up. We can wrap you in this scarf. We will mingle in with next shift. You'll see, it will work!' As a final act of disguise, they popped a screw of old paper in his mouth and set him to masticating, instantly transformed into a gum-chewing American.

The trio ditched what remained of their possessions in the long grass and nettles and strolled casually up to the gate, hands in pockets, shoulders hunched against the cold and breath steaming, timing their arrival with the next grey busload of baby pilots that they gently seeped into. It was clear from the amount of general milling around and the shouted instructions from a flustered man with a clipboard that this was a new intake of fresh, unknown faces. They joined onto the ragtag mob of jostling, joking pupils, all boiling with the excess energy of youth and were led off for processing through the barrier towards a redbrick building that bristled with aerials and, on the way, contrived to dodge behind a stack of sandbags and slip away round the back and towards the hangars, a mere cat's jump away, that gaped so invitingly.

There were various mechanics in navy dungarees, so young as to be possibly also trainees, pottering about in a very relaxed and civilian fashion, uncovering aircraft, checking engine cowlings and tyres, wiping down windscreens from mud and condensation between sips from mugs of tea black with greasy fingerprints. One was washing down a large sign forbidding smoking with a fag in his mouth. Willy liked the look of a spindly, little Miles Magister trainer over in one corner of the hangar - known affectionately as a Maggie - a trim monoplane of spruce and plywood, built as an easy introduction to the Spitfire and Hurricane. It had an open cockpit and would be a bit of a squeeze for three but the controls were rudimentary and unchallenging and it was said to be a most forgiving aircraft to fly.

Otto immediately grasped the situation. Relative age meant that he must be the instructor, the others his charges, and he went up to the fag-puffer exuding the same authority as he would show to a member of the Luftwaffe groundstaff.

'The commandant says can you prepare this aircraft for a training flight. Immediately. I've to take up both students together.' He tweaked three flying helmets off pegs on the wall and flung two casually to Willy and Horst, grabbing a lone pair of goggles for himself.

The boy considered him and stuck out a greasy hand. 'This old kite? You sure? Flight plan?'

'The office isn't open yet. They said they'd send it along.'

The boy shook his head. 'They know we're not allowed to do that.' He threw down the cigarette and crushed the butt underfoot in disgust. 'I've told them a dozen times it's not on. Who was it? Charlie? Tall? Red hair and glasses?'

'I think so.'

'Right. We'll have a bloody word with Charlie.'

He strode across and grabbed a wall-mounted telephone and scowled into the mouthpiece. 'Give me admin.' The silence was electric. They froze and avoided his eyes. Finally, he banged his fist angrily on the wall, leaving a fresh black smear. 'Engaged. Off the bloody hook, like as not. Which is exactly what I won't be if the chief checks up and throws another wobbly.' He hung up bitterly. 'OK. Not your fault I suppose.' Said grudgingly. He pointed at the camouflaged Maggie. 'Take her up, then. We were still working on the old crate but she's airworthy enough and if the commandant says it's OK...But <u>three</u> of you? We've never done that before. Isn't that against regulations?'

Otto put on a rueful expression and shrugged. 'New orders. Something about fuel-saving.'

'Bloody hell. What next? They'll want us to send you up with no bloody engine.' He threw up his hands in despair, very young - Otto thought - to have abandoned all hope of finding sense in the universe but then the military will do that to you.

The three piled in, Willy in front, desperately scanning the controls, Otto and Horst crammed behind, awkwardly sharing a single seat and trying not to look like bolting desperados. The mechanic swung the propeller and the engine coughed into life. As it caught, they could just hear the phone in the hangar start ringing and Willy began gunning the engine and trundling the machine hastily out and towards the runway. The mechanic seemed in no hurry to answer the phone and watched them, headshaking, brow creased with puzzlement and with arms folded. Even if it was the mythical Charlie calling back, they could reckon on a few minutes grace as general confusion and cross-purposes reigned before the shit hit the propeller with any real conviction. But it was important to get up in the air and into that friendly cloud cover before that could happen and the little plane began bobbing down the runway between the now-empty machine gun nests with a din like a frantic petrol lawnmower, each bump like a kick in the bum until the transition from rough ground to smooth air came like a sudden blessing.

♦ ♦ ♦

Billy twirled his stick as he had seen the marine sergeants do and marched the soldiers up to the top of the hill to Candleston Castle on the edge of the dunes like the Grand Old Duke of York. He doubted that he would have the authority to march them down again. It was an old, ruined manor – square and implacable - with high stone walls and tiny, high-set windows and had fallen into disrepair since being abandoned in the 19th century when the restless sea of sand had moved inshore and surrounded it like a besieging army. It was one of their official 'camps' and the boys had defended its ivy-clad stumps many times against imaginary attackers, Red Indians, Normans and Germans. These were always played by the despised evacuee children now purged from the town. That they had brought an epidemic of German measles with them had been the first sign of their doubtful loyalties.

As Billy halted the column outside the main entrance, he was outraged to be firmly pushed to one side and displaced in command. The captain ordered his FFs to fan out, half of them heading for the rear to cut off any retreat, shouting and laughing, but almost shooting each other as they reappeared unannounced round corners and played mutual peek-a-boo over low walls.

Billy shook his head in disbelief. 'Amateurs!' he confided to his men.

The FFs continued to clamber all over the place, waving their rifles, but excitement rapidly gave way to boredom and the exercise petered out into an extended cigarette break, the boys being jokingly offered exotic smokes that were snatched back when accepted. But Billy's troop knew the spot better than anyone. Childhood, like National Socialism, offered regression to a more primitive state of social organisation, with gangs and tribes and a technology of hunters and gatherers. Like aborigines they knew every stone in every path in their territory, every kind of bark and useful branch on every fruiting tree. Taking advantage of wartime neglect, low bushes had invaded the site and nestled up to the crumbling walls and there were clear trails through them that had not been there before and shuffling, nocturnal rustlings in broad daylight. The FFs had ignored them, reluctant to get their trousers wet from the rainfall of the previous night that still clung to their leaves. Billy marched up to the captain, boldly seized his embroidered sleeve and pointed.

'There!'

'Eh?' He looked contemptuously, shook him off disdainfully. 'Is nothing. Rabbits, maybe.' And went back to blowing rich, aromatic smoke.

'There!' he screamed. 'I know this place. There's been people there and no one ever comes but me and my gang. I know what I'm saying. I'm not talking bosh.'

'What? Boches! Les boches? Òu ça?' It was a magic word - like the word for food to a dog. Ears were pricked, cigarettes flung to the ground, limbs stiffened and the troops were immediately back on their feet, bright-eyed, rooting joyfully, trampling down Nature, prodding with rifles and crushing the branches to reveal the threat of three frightened men, looking like Worzel Gummidges and cowering in the undergrowth with raised hands. 'Boches! Boches! On a trouvé des boches!'

'Aha! Les boches!' The captain swaggered up to them and smirked, slapping his hand down on the shoulder of the largest with a firm 'Thwack!' and pushing his face up really close. 'I arrest you in the name of Général de Gaulle! You are a prisoner of France!'

Then, he pivoted on one heel, snapped to attention and executed a sharp salute of acknowledgment to Billy and his gang. They nearly swooned with excitement.

♦ ♦ ♦

'The problem is we haven't got any charts in this cursed plane. There's all sorts of other junk up here and I hoped there might be some maps somewhere but here's absolute <u>Scheisse</u>. And this compass is worse than the ones we made ourselves back in the camp. With this thick cloud cover, I just don't know where we are.'

Willy peered despairingly over the side of the aircraft which had shown itself far from being in apple-pie order, actually more an apple-pie bed. In fact, the rotten, old machine was nothing but a deathtrap which is probably why it had been half dumped in the hangar in the first place. Some of the instrumentation was blatantly out of commission, which cast suspicion on any claims to authority made by the rest. The alleged airspeed was implausible without rocket assistance and Willy's calculations on how far they could get if the fuel gauge was anywhere near accurate were made approximate again by the extra weight of a third passenger. Anyway, when you tapped on the glass of the fuel indicator, the needle went confidently from 'full' to 'empty' and then gaily back again. The truth, it seemed to say, lay somewhere or other – anywhere really, take your choice - in between.

They had finally got the Gosport speaking tube working and could talk to each other above the deafening engine. Shivering in the bitter cold and wet despite bunched up greatcoats, they had come down as low as they dared to try to get out of the clammy grip of icy fog and gain some sort of visual fix on where they might be. Lower, lower. The air stank of some foul industrial effluent trapped under the clouds. Then suddenly the veil of fog was torn apart, demystified, to give a view such as Willy might have dreamed of in his warlike days. Lots of the Luftwaffe pilots fitted illegal cameras to their own aircraft to document their dogfights. Of course, his own would have been facing in the wrong direction to pick out the Hurricane that shot him down but this panorama would have given some great vistas to show in the mess. A huge river estuary stretched out down there, dotted with the great belching, industrial chimneys of fat, inviting targets. It lay all neatly spread out and almost sexually vulnerable beneath them and, beyond it, a vast plain of water, flat and the colour of steel, gleaming off to the west with a fragment of noon sun glinting on its surface.

'The sea! The Irish sea!' Horst and Otto shouted excitedly like children on a trip to the seaside as they caught their first sight of the beach.

'Right,' said Willy, cutting through their joy like a parent refusing ice cream and insisting on the eating of greens. He throttled the engine back to a dull roar and began the little speech he had been rehearsing for the past hour. It was uncomfortable, looking forward and talking to people behind your back. You couldn't see their faces, couldn't tell how they were taking it. 'This is how it is. We don't know how much fuel we have. We don't know what our fuel consumption is. We don't know our speed. I would guess we're doing 150 kph with no headwind. We don't know where we are, so we don't know how far it is across the sea to Ireland and if we can even make it that far. If we head due west, we should sooner or later hit land that's part of the Republic, not Northern Ireland – unless we miss it entirely and have to fly all the way to America, that is. Alternatively, we could look for another airstrip and try to bluff them into refuelling the plane and hope they don't join up all the dots and arrest us so we end up back in the camp. What do you want me to do? You decide.'

♦ ♦ ♦

CHAPTER TEN

The familiar voice of Winston Churchill spluttered out over the airwaves, the vowels creaking, the consonants reduced to a fuzzy blur. 'Yesterday morning at 2.41 am, at General Eisenhower's headquarters, General Jodl, the representative of the German High Command, and of Grand Admiral Dönitz, the designated head of the German state, signed the act of unconditional surrender of all German land, sea and air forces in Europe to the Allied Expeditionary Forces and simultaneously to the Soviet High Command. Hostilities will end officially at one minute after midnight tonight, Tuesday the eighth of May...We may allow ourselves a brief period of rejoicing; but let us not forget for a moment the toil and efforts that lie ahead. Japan with all her treachery and greed, remains unsubdued...We must now devote all our strength and resources to the completion of our task, both at home and abroad. Advance Britannia! Long live the cause of freedom! God save the King!'

◆ ◆ ◆

Superintendent May stood in the door of his office and glared. It was that greasy and anonymous little man from Security again, the one who had trampled on his washing lines plan, sitting there with frowsy mackintosh retained, and scratching his crotch without inhibition, smoking and flicking the ash on the floor as if it was his own patch. He went round to the other side of his desk and set down his hat carefully and sat primly, saying nothing.

'Good news, super.' Security man winked and tapped his nose conspiratorially and quite horribly. 'The mandarins in Whitehall have held their little enquiry, in secret of course, and a certain document will ultimately be produced – with necessary omissions – and circulated but I can safely leak the result.' He looked the sort of man who might well leak something. 'Good news for you.'

Superintendent May frowned. No one had told him. No one had asked him to give evidence. 'An enquiry? Into the escape? But isn't that a little premature? After all, we haven't even recaptured them all yet.' He reached across and rattled his biscuit tin like a Salvation Army lady her tambourine. A lazy scratching noise confirmed his claim. He opened the lid and displayed the contents. There were still three little swastika flags in there, peeking out, looking for a home.

'Your name and the swift and successful outcome of the manhunt have been noted by a certain person of eminence and you may confidently expect to see yourself included on a certain list in the new year.'

'A list? What list? What on earth is all this about? I keep telling you, it's not done and dusted yet. There are still three escapees on the loose.'

'For you, superintendent, ze hunt is ofer.' Said with a fake, hammy German accent. 'We are drawing a line. Things have moved on. The Jerries are being rounded up bit by bit. What with the Ruskies in Berlin and our own troops moving across to join them, it's all over bar the shouting. No one is interested in looking backwards. There are other challenges now. As you know, the camp at Bridgend has already been cleared and will be repurposed. All prisoners have been accounted for. That's straight from the highest level and I'm getting the same clear message thrown at me whichever way I look.' He flung himself back and from side to side in his chair, rolled his eyes and covered his face, reeling against imaginary blows from all sides.

'But they haven't all been recaptured...'

'I didn't say "recaptured". I repeat. With millions of lost people wandering about all over the world, officially, all prisoners have been accounted for - within the limits of acceptable error.' He took the tin from May's desk, opened the lid again and gently tipped it up so that the contents were sent spiralling down into the wastepaper basket, twirling like sycamore seeds doomed to fall on stony ground.

May protested. 'But the whole thing was the most enormous shambles. You didn't see the prisoners leaving when they closed the camp. I did. They marched off whistling and laughing as if they had got the better of us all. For them, it was some huge joke. It should never have been allowed to happen. Do we just pretend it never did happen?'

Security man yawned and stretched. 'As I said, lessons have been learned, Mr. Growser, multiple improvements have already been implemented. The whole matter has been brought to a successful conclusion and filed away – in secret files naturally. But now we've got tens of thousands of our own prisoners being released across Europe and clamouring for repatriation. New problems, new responsibilities.'

'Repurposed, you said? The camp. Well, I hope they don't stick our lads in there when they get them out of Jerry PoW camps. There are rumours. That would be just too cruel. I've seen pictures in the newspapers of their starved, haunted faces. They deserve better than that, the best food, a taste of town life, getting back to their families, getting them home. I imagine it'll take a while for their back pay to come through but still... I suppose it might give a real boost to the local economy. People here have suffered terribly too, you know.'

Security man laughed, showing nicotine-stained teeth. 'You don't know the half of it – and even the half of it isn't what they'll actually get. Now they've had a nice war, the bills are coming in and the citizens get to pay for it – with full service charge added. Under the terms of the Geneva Convention...' May's head swirled. '...believe it or not, our own PoWs get docked a third of their back pay for the crappy food and accommodation they got under the Jerries and that cash goes straight to the piggy bank of our vanquished foes. The Jerry trusties over here got paid in real money at union rates for their work on the farms and some have got a nice little sum tucked away, tax free, whereas our boys can get charged for kit lost when they surrendered and still get taxed on the whole initial sum. A neat racket played by the numbers boys but the squaddies won't like it when they find out. We haven't even begun to see the social consequences of this war as yet. There's a revolution coming.' He shrugged and flicked ash. 'More work for me, I suppose,' May bit down on the sour words he was about to utter. 'Oh, and I forgot. By the way, your masonic chum, Lieutenant Colonel Darling...'

'Yes?' May looked up, concerned. 'Edwin? He genuinely did his best, you know. It really wasn't all his fault. I do hope they weren't too hard on him.' Poor Edwin, he was more sensitive than people realised and always took criticism so to heart. Half the trouble was that silly, stuck-up English accent that people here read as plummy arrogance riding on the coat tails of privilege. He felt tears in his eyes.

The Security man laughed. 'You might say that, old man, though the last time I saw him he had that permanently worried look of the man in the insurance advert who suddenly realised his job wasn't pensionable.' He blew smoke. 'Look, it's still in the pipeline but the word is Darling's been promoted and put in overall charge of security inspections in every single PoW camp across the UK. Don't worry about him. Greatness beckons. He'll be farting through silk.' He whistled, stubbed out his cigarette and smirked. 'Now our eyes turn east. Don't you know there's still a war on?'

May found absolutely nothing to say to that. You could hear a pin drop. He stared down bitterly at his three little flags in the waste basket, upended in mute appeal, legs in the air like helpless maybugs tipped on their backs. He closed his tin with a final snap and dropped it onto them.

◆ ◆ ◆

They stuck to following the sun due west. With thick cloud cover, there was no alternative and Willy noted with irritation the way the compass danced around, taking delight in pointing any which way, trying to lead them astray. The little trainer was not built for the higher altitudes where fuel consumption would have been better. They would have frozen to death up there, so they stayed just above the cloud level, ready to dive into it if anything like an RAF plane appeared on the horizon. As it was, Otto and Horst found themselves almost losing consciousness from the cold and Willy sang to himself to keep awake as he watched his hands on the controls turn from pink to dark blue and all feeling fled from his fingers.

He looked at the swirling balls of water vapour and found himself thinking about his mother's <u>Lebkuchen</u>, Christmas biscuits lush with ginger and treacle, and of a fight he had had with his brothers where they had thrown them at each other over the festive table in selfish rage and ingratitude. Well, no spicy <u>Lebkuchen</u> now, so soft on the tongue, no brothers any more. Perhaps no mother. His head nodded and he was dipping down into sleep when the engine coughed and he jerked awake and hiccupped up the ghostly crumbs of biscuit he had tasted in his semi-dream. The engine coughed again. He hit the fuel gauge. It stayed stuck on empty. Its wandering days were over – it seemed to say – and so were theirs. With a final rasp the engine died and the hissing rush of the air was suddenly the only sound beating against the cockpit as the nose dipped and they plunged down into the cloud as into a tunnel.

'What's happening? What's going on?' Otto and Horst were screaming in the intercom. Willy was unsurprised by his own coolness.

'Strap yourselves in as best you can. We're coming in to land.'

And then they were through the cloud and beneath them there was nothing but empty water, no land at all.

'Take off those overcoats and dump the boots. We're going to have to swim.'

It was a restless and unwelcoming military sea, khaki green, steely blue with patches of hard, <u>Wehrmacht</u> grey and no sign of a coastline anywhere. And then they saw a finger smear of white, the wake of a ship, looking completely lost out here and their hearts soared as the plane plunged. If they were to die, at least they would not die alone.

Willy circled around the vessel like an indecisive mosquito, slowing, dropping down, as figures crowded onto the deck, waving and shouting, pointing at the Irish tricolour hitched to the stern. It was a tiny fishing vessel, wooden built, with a small deckhouse painted blue and white. They could see mouths opening and closing but without sound as in a silent film as the boat glided under them. It occurred to Willy that they thought they were coming in for an attack. Because of the clouds, they cast no shadow. The sea rose up to meet them far too fast, but at the last minute, Willy managed to raise the nose of the Maggie and arrange a wet bellyflop on a rising wave as the plane stalled and a wall of icy water cascaded through it with a screeching of splintered wood. The wing on one side sheared off and they began to spin and found themselves washed through the hole and out into a tossing sea with Horst holding up a limp Uncle Otto with a great gash on his forehead. The advantages of a wooden plane, built like a giant version of a little boy's balsa wood model, were now self-evident as it bobbed on the surface, the waves licking at it with no dangerous undertow as it sank. Horst kicked clear and tried not to think of the miles of cold, empty water, home to thousands of the bleached corpses of sailors, beneath them. Willy – raised on Jules Verne - tried hard not to think of what might be alive in the turbid depths and looking up hungrily at their juicy, flailing legs.

◆ ◆ ◆

'So who are you then?'

Billy was not in the least intimidated any more by the figures behind the barbed wire of the camp, German big brass, tinkling with symbols of rank. They had changed the name of the place but it was still Jerries in there and this was still the same cluster of buildings of a joyless ugliness that was recognisably masculine. Yet this was palpably a different sort of German. What had once been described as caged tigers were now just limping bunny rabbits, like that character in the Wizard of Oz that hid behind a curtain of intimidation. There was none of the spitting and screaming and waving of fists of the past. None of the danger and excitement either. Where once battleready youths had performed glittering gymnastic feats, a bunch of elderly gentlemen now pottered in subdued fashion like in one of the aspidistra-dotted seaside retirement homes down by the coast. True, there were no boaters and stripy blazers here but plenty of pocket badges and hats suitable for yachting in and, with the reduction in population, something approaching a lawn had been coaxed into existence between the bleak huts.

The little, old man in the navyblue overcoat was sitting on an upturned box right by a fencepost and leaning against the very wire, a walking stick stowed between his legs, a cushion tucked under his bony rump, taking a little sun and staring out wistfully. He looked Billy evenly in the face and their eyes locked. He beckoned the boy across with thin, blue hands that retained a hint of trembling impatience but there was a twinkle in his eyes that belied the frailty of his body and, when Billy got close, his breath smelled of something spicy and alcoholic or perhaps it was that the coat had just been dry-cleaned and not aired properly as Mum said it had to be or you would catch cancer and die. They never would have let prisoners get so close to the fence before but this one was clearly not about to leap onto the box and jump over it. Boots of a supernatural sheen and elegance peeped out from beneath the coat.

'Who am I? My name is Gerd von Rundstedt, young man. General Field Marshal Gerd von Rundstedt.' The very name was a performance, said not without pride, an 'r' like a military drumroll, a truculent forward motion of the chin, a smile and a raising of the brow as if anticipating instant recognition or even applause. 'Name, rank and serial number are all I am obliged to tell you as my interrogator. Would you like to know my serial number?'

Billy frowned. He only knew serial numbers as something bad that got you caught on stolen banknotes at the pictures and good on electric irons when you took them back to the shop because they weren't working and they wanted to wriggle out of the guarantee.

'No thank you, sir. Is this where you live now then?'

The old man sighed. 'For the moment, it seems. It is not quite the Georges V in Paris or the Palace Hotel in Luxembourg, though there is talk of my going to Nuremberg. There are very good hotels there, I recall, though I avoided those horrible rallies.'

Billy knew all about Nuremberg. It was in all the papers and people didn't go there for the fine hotels. That was where the trials for war crimes lived. The endless long words. The elaborate posturing in the papers by vicars and politicians. His dad's solution to the moral knots they were tying themselves in - fresh back from the war and delivered at the wireless over the breakfast table sauce bottles - had been incisive, 'Shoot the bloody lot and we could spare a few of the buggers who were on our side and all.' Dad had been coarsened by the military. He said less, drank more and was given to outbursts of rage and socialism that the family had learned to tread round lightly.

'Nuremberg? What did you do?'

The old man stiffened and considered. 'Well, I suppose I invaded Poland and France and Russia and fought on the Atlantic Wall and the Ardennes Offensive – what you call the Battle of the Bulge.' He changed tack. 'Your father was in the war?'

'He served on the Orkneys front.'

'The Orkneys? Was there a great battle there? I do not recollect it. Some people find being the senior commander of the German army hard to forgive but it is a soldier's duty to obey orders even when he knows they will turn out badly. I'm sure you do what you are told by your parents and teachers even when you may not want to and doubt their wisdom.'

'They told me not to come here but I did anyway.'

He laughed. 'Perhaps you are right but I was not raised that way. We had cold baths and lots of beatings at the school for cadets. I suppose I might have shot myself when the American army came for me at the spa. I thought about it. There were... precedents. The walls are all tiled and can be washed, so it would have caused small inconvenience, but that would have suggested I had a reason for shame and put me in bad company since a lot of guilty people were shooting themselves at that time. Even before the war, the other generals kept whispering to me and saying, "Let's get rid of the little corporal. Like Napoleon, you know? Do it for Germany." We were all aristos of proper family and had married each other for generations and had been to the same military academies but I always refused. I didn't...sneak – is that the word? – on them as I'm sure you would not but I never took part in any of that dirty business. Then, of course, the little corporal kept firing me every time I proved him wrong in the field. He was a silly, little man and really quite common. I retired three times but he forced me back into my harness, every time. This time I think it is final and I am sure to have the last word.' He sighed like someone loosening a constricting tie after a night out. 'The strange thing is, my young friend, when a great disaster happens, like losing a world war for example, you remain completely calm. It is the little things that one continues to worry about.'

'The little things?' Billy had no grandfather but he felt, perhaps for the first time, that he would have liked one. Fathers were too remote. A natural embarrassment existed between them and their sons. He would never be able to talk to his father like this. They would say it was the war had done that too, that had separated them at a formative stage, but it was really just the way of the world.

'Yes.' The field marshal leaned forward and dropped his voice, as if conveying some great war secret. 'Do you know? Half the generals here, lower in rank than myself of course, eat with Other Ranks although that is contrary to regular usage and they even allow the SS in here with us, loathsome bugs that they are. Of course, I have asked for them to be removed. I am reduced to having a single manservant and the guards here make themselves anxious over stupid regulations that forbid us to wear our military decorations.' He pulled back his collar defiantly to show some sort of fancy medal around his neck and rattled his cane against his box. 'Once I carried a gold field marshal's baton, now I have just a wooden stick to help me walk.' He smashed the handle of it viciously against the wire. A squaddie looked up, frowning at the noise, then looked away. 'Once I invaded continents, now I have to ask permission to go to town and buy socks and they expect me to – what is the word? – make a snake - queue! Me! But the beds here are terribly hard for an old man. In the old days, I was the only general who did not have to stand up in the little corporal's presence. He used to make that great slug Göring get up and offer me his seat! But can you believe it? – they brought us here in a <u>third class</u> railway carriage! Not even second class. When we may all end up being shot next week, there is no reason for this inhumane treatment. Third class! Even my Iron Cross is <u>first</u> class.'

The myths that had sustained him through the years did not lie buried in the rubble of a Berlin he had helped to destroy so much as under the hard seats and among the heating pipes of the Great Western Railway.

Perhaps grandfathers were no better than fathers, after all. 'There is no second class on the railways, Mr. Fon...It's first or third with nothing in between.'

'Is that possible, young man?' He popped his eyes at the wonder of it. 'That is like going from lieutenant to corporal with no sergeant in between. It makes no sense.' He grumbled to himself. 'But I suppose nothing much makes sense any more. Do you know what they are threatening to do to us now? They want to throw us out of the army so that we cease to be prisoners of war, then they can confiscate our pensions as well as prosecuting us. They have frozen my bank account. The Russians have seized my estate. Human dignity is incompatible with extreme poverty, my young friend. Never forget that. It is more likely to break a man than physical torture because it destroys who he knows himself to be. I have taken to painting. The walls here, even those of the old gymnasium, are decorated with pictures in the most appalling taste or works of blatant Nazi propaganda and I can't bear to look at them. So I have to show them how it's done but I can barely afford paint these days. Can you believe they pay a former field marshal £16 a month – and in useless camp money.'

Billy did not know what to make of that. For him, half a crown was barely imaginable wealth.

'I have seen you in the past, with your friends, beyond the wire. Where are they today?'

'They've been reassigned.' It was a word much used of late. Jimmy's father had been shifted to the fruitless evangelisation of a seedy part of Swansea inhabited by determinedly Muslim Malay sailors, Arthur's dad had resumed criminal activities and the family was enjoying what would surely be a brief period of flashy financial exuberance in London. Fred's mother had just married a strutting, newly-promoted Captain Wilson from the camp and been posted to the garrison in Hong Kong. There was a joke doing the rounds. 'Poor? After the war we were so poor we had to have my baby brother made in Hong Kong.' For poor Fred, joke had become fact. And now Billy's men had gone and faded away into the peace just like von Rundstedt's ghostly legions and he was alone too. No joke.

◆ ◆ ◆

The three men were hauled up on deck like fresh-caught whales and lay, coughing, in pools of seawater and shivering with cold. The crew seemed to be three men, burly, hirsute, dark-eyed and bearded – a bit like the dog men back at the camp – and a scrawny, ferret-faced cabin boy. The stink of fish was everywhere. They spoke to each other, back and forth, in a soft, unknown tongue that sounded like the wind in long grass. They clearly came to some sort of conclusion as they bent and shouldered the three, one by one, into the little cabin and the lad set to making tea, offered up spiked with some fiery spirit that made them cough still more.

'English?' said the man who must be the skipper.

They looked at each other, hesitated, wondered what was best to say, realised they could not carry it off.

'Dutch,' said Otto. 'Dutch Air Force.'

'It was an English plane. So you are fighting for the English, then, which is the same thing?' There was an interchange in the rustling-grass language of the Gaeltacht and he turned with a suddenly hard face. 'We do not greatly like the English. The English burned our village during the Troubles. The English killed my brother.'

'A misunderstanding,' Otto amended swiftly. 'Not Dutch. My English is not good. Deutsch – German. We are German prisoners of war and we capitulate ourselves to you.'

The skipper held out a sodden piece of paper, the ink running. 'There was this fell from your pocket.' It was one of the fake Dutch identity cards. 'It was an English plane,' he said again and turned away as if that was the end of the matter.

They never learned the name of the village. Every time they asked, it seemed to change. They were sure the children, at least, were doing it deliberately. As they were first led up from a scrap of beach, a gang of the ragged urchins in great, clumping boots accompanied them, shouting and dancing in and out of the road before the procession. The ferret-faced cabin boy was led off by his peers for interrogation. The villagers stared at them with hard, closed faces, the women folding their arms across their chests in that universal sign of female disapproval of anything from the outside. A low inn crouched above the sea and the men all crowded in, the women being left outside. The door closed and the howl of wind was cut off. Otto, Horst and Willy, were seated at a rough table, a glass of the lethal spirit was set before them and they were ignored.

The skipper held the floor, clearly giving his account of events in a dramatic performance with a dancer's gestures that drew 'oohs' and 'aahs' from the audience. At one point he leapt on the table and then dived to the floor, spinning on one foot.

'That would be the crash-landing,' Otto observed.

'I did not crash. I made a perfect landing – only there was no land.' Willy was firm.

The skipper straightened his hat, tucked his thumbs under imaginary lapels and waltzed across the floor in a hoity-toity fashion.

'That would be Uncle Otto surrendering in English,' said Willy.

The skipper flung himself across a table, rolled his eyes and let his tongue loll out and made noises like a seal asking for fish at the circus. The audience roared with laughter.

'That would be the boat journey home.'

The meeting lapsed into a general discussion at which some got more angry than might have seemed possible. The Germans sat quietly, assuming the least provocative expressions they could. Otto went for 'benign schoolmasterly', the other two 'polite young boy scouts', until some sort of a reluctant consensus was reached, at which the innkeeper's wife appeared at the door and beckoned them away up a rattly staircase and into a low, dark room with one enormous, lumpy bed. She was a lumpy, silent woman herself with a large bunch of keys, whose frustrated destiny was to be a prison wardress. They fell on to the bed and were asleep in seconds. As she went out, she locked the door behind her.

◆ ◆ ◆

After the first night, they had been allowed to roam much as they liked, the children keeping some sort of a check on what they might be up to and the only real interest they aroused was in the innkeeper's dog, a large, normally phlegmatic beast, that whined with pleasure at the sight of Willy and rushed across to thrust its massive head in his lap. They cultivated its affection as a mark of their common humanity.

It was a bleak and treeless place with a semi-permanent gale that roared in from the Atlantic as in a wind tunnel and a wild sea that crashed against the rocks in pointless fury. The rocks were clothed in hunched and bitter plants, clinging on for dear life. It reminded Otto of Wenke turned magically into landscape. The smaller boats were of a weird construction of cowhide stretched over a wooden frame, as frail as flesh over old ladies' bones and, unsurprisingly, the cemetery boasted the headstones of few past the age of fifty. It was a place of small delights and only one or two of the men even spoke much English.

At noon, the door was flung open. Caught by the gusting wind, it crashed back against the wall with a noise like a thunderclap and a figure in black stepped through and paused, the light glinting off his glasses. SS! No a priest with his black soutane flapping in the Atlantic gale! Father O'Flaherty was a man of some sophistication, having trained at a Dublin seminary where they taught him to spot the disguises of the Devil as ruthlessly as in the courses of aircraft silhouette identification that Willy had undergone in the Luftwaffe. He came and sat silently at their table, laying down a hat like a waiter serving a dish of food. The other occupants of the room hushed and seemed to fall back. It was clear who made all the decisions around here. The innkeeper hustled over with a glass of the usual dry-cleaning fluid.

The priest looked around the group like a hawk in a nest of titmice. His wire-rimmed glasses, astride a great turnip of a nose cut forensically through any artifice.

'You are English,' he said and raised eyebrows like two great, spiky caterpillars. It was less a question than an accusation. To atone for it would be three Hail Marys at least.

'No, we are German.'

'Do not lie to me. The plane was English.'

'We stole the plane. We are German prisoners of war.'

'You also said you were Dutch.'

'A misunderstanding. There was a language difficulty.'

'Your papers said you were Dutch.'

'We wrote our own papers in order to escape.'

The priest sucked at his whisky like a someone sucking on a snakebite. 'The Germans made us promises but they did not keep them, like the politicians did not keep theirs and signed that shameful treaty with the English. We were betrayed. A while back there was a submarine that came offshore. When we went out to meet it, expecting arms (or was it alms?) they sank one of our boats, an innocent fishing boat that was doing no harm. Some of the men here who thought you were German wanted to take you out to sea and drown you for that. Others wanted to kill you for being Dutch collaborators with the English or maybe being English yourselves. You might think it is a strange kind of active neutrality we have here where we fight with everyone. But then we also fight with each other so there is a certain justice in it.'

Otto was the only one who spoke this priestly tongue, summoning up the ghost of his days at that Catholic boys' school. 'As a man of the cloth, you surely could not go along with that?'

'In a war, my son, you have to hang on to the greater cause while being flexible in little matters. Now, a man's life is not a little thing but neither is a people's freedom. We learnt that in the days of the Republic of Munster, during the civil war, and some of our bishops who support the government from their fine palaces now would do well to remember it.' He had warmed his hands at many a blazing Georgian country house at the time, the dry, ancient beams and fine, oak panelling sending up rejoicing sparks into the night sky. Oil paintings went up particularly well.

'Münster is in Germany.'

Father O'Flaherty suffered contradiction ill. He was not used to it in his village. He raised his voice. 'Munster is an ancient kingdom of Ireland where we are now and you would do well not to forget it. It is carved in the hearts of the people of this place.'

Otto did not like the way this was going but ancient memories stirred of how he would ingratiate himself with the fathers at school, sometimes even avoiding a harsh beating with the leather tawse by confessing to some more interesting titbit of evil that they could thunder and posture about. 'I should dearly like to make my confession to you father. It has been several years since I have had the chance and my breaking of the Lord's commandments lies heavy on my soul.'

Father O'Flaherty brightened and flared his nostrils, smelling a rich dish of exotic sin being served up for the tasting. The venial offences of the villagers offered little opportunity to stretch himself – the same dreary crimes, endlessly repeated, of drunkenness and fornication spiced up with the odd bit of old sea folklore that he could reasonably call 'worshipping the devil' in his sermons.

'You are of the faith? Then let us go upstairs immediately and purge the devil out of you, my son.' He drained his glass with relish and banged it down on the table. He liked nothing so much as a good bareknuckle fight with the ultimate old enemy.

They were gone some time and occasionally from below they heard raised voices and the sound of someone beating rhythmically as with a fist on furniture. There came a crash of some heavy object hitting the floor, then the sound of boots clattering on the bare stairs and Father O'Flaherty stalked out, skirts swirling, looking neither to right nor left but grim-jawed and with eyes aflame.

Uncle Otto reappeared red-faced and resumed his seat. No one spoke.

Finally, he said, 'Perhaps I went a bit far. I just imagined myself in Wenke's boots and dumped the lot on him. It's hard to shock a priest and I knew I had to. He says we can leave at the end of the week when there should be transport, in fact he insists on it, but, if I were you, I shouldn't be caught talking to any of the local ladies before then. On the good side, my theology's a little rusty nowadays, but it's just possible Wenke might now scrape into Heaven – by proxy.'

◆ ◆ ◆

The inspector from the Irish Special Branch shuffled papers on the battle-scarred desk and made a face. He had sad eyes and reeked of Bay Rum hair tonic. The tonic wasn't working and, at the temples, recession showed, so perhaps it was just a way of hiding the quick one he had taken in the cloakroom to fortify himself before the interview. He cleared his throat. 'So the idea is you lads want to surrender yourselves to me and claim asylum in the Republic of Ireland as escaped German prisoners of war.' He flung down his pencil. 'I'll be honest with you. I'm afraid it's not quite that simple. In fact, it's a devil of a time to be turning up like this. Couldn't you just go away for a couple of months and come back later?'

The three men looked both dismayed and astonished.

'After all, I've no way of confirming your story. The English say all their escaped prisoners were recaptured. You say you ditched a stolen British aeroplane in the drink off the coast but there's no evidence of that, do you see? You're not on any list. And you're not in any kind of uniform, are you?' He gestured towards their thick knit pullovers and workmen's trousers and boots.

Not this again. 'The trawlermen who rescued us gave us clothes and burned ours because they were full of lice. We only have our flying helmets.' Otto laid one gently on the desk.

Special Branch groped for his pencil and poked at it as if it, too, were full of lice and shook his head. 'A hat? Is that it? All you can show me is a hat like some saint's relic? Also, it's a British flyer's helmet. Not German. German would have been better for your story, you know.'

'The plane was British. It came with the plane,' Willy protested. 'You would not get a German hat in a British plane.'

'Look, I'll be completely frank with you lads. There's been a terrible cock-up in Dublin. Not your fault of course but not mine either. No one knows what the hell is going on. The European war is over though we're not even supposed to use that word as neutrals. It's always 'the situation in Europe' for us. If you'd only come a little bit earlier, everything would have been so much simpler.

Horst chimed in. 'We couldn't come earlier. The trawler carried us off to some arschloching island way down south and we had no idea where we even were. They were kind, of course, but it took forever to get back to the mainland. We were trapped in a tiny village and it was terribly dull and we ate nothing but cabbage and potatoes, day after day. It made me homesick for my holidays in Schleswig Holstein. And then...'

Special Branch threw up his hands. He could not take such complaints seriously. In his experience of the Black and Tans, armies were like mindless swarms of locusts that settled indifferently on a community, fed, procreated and flitted on with their last gasp, belch and bowel movement. 'Yes, yes. They're a difficult lot down there and they don't like us Garda very much. Did you happen to catch the names of any of the people there?'

Otto blinked. 'The names didn't make any sense to us. It was as if they didn't have vowels.'

'Well, as you will know, we are still neutral but at the start of things, when British boys ended up here, we just sent them back without any bother. Then, your lads started washing ashore in numbers and we had to intern the lot of you both just to be fair. Principle of moral equivalence. You can see that? So we used to send you along to the Curragh where we kept the IRA hard-liners who were so keen on your Nazi leaders, thinking you'd all get along. But certain individuals got it in their heads that there should be a difference between prisoners and internees and then they got the wind up about the English press and the Germans were very pushy, so belligerents got given pocket money and were all shoved out on parole and had a gay old time what with trips to Dublin and all. So then, we just let the Brits go on the quiet, creep back across the border, no names no pack drill, while we looked the other way and you Jerries were allowed to move to Dublin full time and enrol in educational courses and the like and live the life of harmless, scruffy students. Then people found out your lot were being allowed to get unlimited drink duty-free at the camp and were selling it off in Dublin, undercutting the wholesalers and making a bloody fortune while having high jinks with the ladies and laying out your rent in kind, if you get my meaning. The newspapers made a meal of that and the government ended up looking very foolish.' A bad time. He was sweating at the mere memory of it.

The three men, on the other hand, perked up visibly. Drink, women, money! That didn't sound too bad – a lot better than cabbage and potatoes. A wild city where they kept the lights on at night. Willy had been briefed on using the lights of the South to guide the bombers into targets in the North. The Irish were supposed to be the perennially rainsodden people who added dissolute fire to an otherwise stodgy empire. A little of that would go a long way.

'But then there was that business in Dresden and the government got all uppity with the English again and things started to happen so fast that we just couldn't keep up with events any more. It's a shambles. The government shouldn't have trotted along to the German embassy and said they were so sorry to hear it when your Mr. Hitler died. Some of our own people didn't care for that at all and the English disliked him shooting his own dog the way he did. Now, a few weeks back, we could have just notified the German authorities and shipped the lot of you off to Dublin and washed our hands of it but now there is no Third Reich any more for them to be authorities of and no German minister either, so we don't know what the hell to do with you. You're not officially here at all. I'm afraid you're an administrative anomaly lads, in limbo, and there's damn all I can do for you without a bit of divine intervention. When I was a child, the priests used to tell us most folks in limbo just sit and pray to the saints for their swift deliverance and perhaps that helps but then I'm not much of a god-fearing man myself.'

'But what should we do? Where can we go? Surely you have to at least arrest us for something?' Otto had an idea. 'If we punched you in the face, would that help?'

'Well now. Steady on. Don't go upsetting yourselves.' A cunning gleam came into his eye. He leaned forward and lowered his voice. 'I've got a chum in the English Security Service in London who shall remain nameless. You might say we're the best of enemies. But he owes me one for sending him the weather reports from the far west – you know your lot used to have to try to reconstruct what weather was blowing your way by listening to English and Irish football matches on the wireless? We had to say it was sunny when it was pouring with rain.' He laughed. 'Well, I've had a word on the blower and he's prepared to be flexible for once. It's all fixed. We can give you a ride up north and slip you across the border and he'll arrange for his men to smuggle you into Gosford PoW Camp up in County Armagh. Let him have your details and he'll shuffle round all the paperwork so it looks like a regular transfer from where you were before and then you can be repatriated with no fuss in due course like everyone else. How's that now?'

'You mean we'll end up back in a British camp, just sitting about again and waiting to go home?'

'Yes, but it's rather a nice little camp up there as such things go. Peaceful, though I hear there's a few mosquitoes at this time of year. But I wouldn't mention our own little arrangement to anyone else if I were you or they'll think you're spies and that can be quite nasty.'

'You mean we've gone through all this just to end up back where we started?'

Special Branch sucked on his teeth and looked even sadder. 'Afraid so. But that's the whole story of the past few years isn't it? At least you haven't lost anything. You're no worse off, are you? You've had a nice little jaunt and got new pullovers and what else can we do? Don't you know there's a war on?' He slapped his hand to his mouth. 'Oops! Actually there isn't, is there? At least not here. But you know what I mean.'

◆ ◆ ◆

Printed in Great Britain
by Amazon